RELINQUISH

By: International Bestselling Author
Sapphire Knight

Relinquish
Copyright © 2017 by Sapphire Knight

Cover Design by CT Cover Creations
Editing by Mitzi Carroll
Formatting by Formatting Done Wright

ALSO BY SAPPHIRE

Oath Keepers MC Series

Secrets
Exposed
Relinquish
Forsaken Control
Friction
Princess
Sweet Surrender – free short story
Daydream

Russkaya Mafiya Series

Secrets
Corrupted
Unwanted Sacrifices
Undercover Intentions
Russian Roulette

Standalones

Gangster
Unexpected Forfeit
1st Time Love

WARNING

This novel includes graphic language and adult situations. It may be offensive to some readers and includes situations that may be hotspots for certain individuals. This book is intended for ages 18 and older due to some steamy spots. This work is fictional. The story is meant to entertain the reader and may not always be completely accurate. Any reproduction of these works without Author Sapphire Knight's written consent is pirating and will be punished to the fullest extent of the law.

ACKNOWLEDGEMENTS

My husband and cover model Jamie Knight- I love you more than words can express. Thank you for the support you've shown me. Somedays you drive me crazy, other days I just want to kiss your face off. Who knew this would turn out to be our life, but in this journey, I wouldn't want to spend it with anyone else. Thanks for falling for my brand of crazy. Thank you for putting up with my shenanigans and killing yourself in the gym so I can have you on my book cover. I'd take you anyway, however, because you're beautiful in my eyes all the time. I love you, I'm thankful for you, I can't say it enough.

My boys - You are my whole world. I love you both. This never changes, and you better not be reading these books until you're thirty and tell yourself your momma did not write them! I can never express how grateful I am for your support. You are quick to tell me that my career makes you proud, that I make you proud. As far as mom wins go; that one takes the cake. I love you with every beat of my heart and I will forever.

Editor Mitzi Carroll – You're one of the most dedicated, kindest people I've come across in this industry. I will forever be grateful that J.C. Valentine suggested I ask for your help. I was lost at a time in my career and you literally jumped in and saved me. I will never forget that or how much you've helped me grow since then. You are a true gem and I look forward to finally getting to hug you in Cincinnati! Your hard work makes mine stand out, and I'm so grateful! Thank you for pouring tons of hours into my passion and being so wonderful to me.

Cover Designer CT Cover Creations – You blow me away with each design! I don't know how you do it, but you render me speechless over and over. I cannot thank you enough for the wonderful work you've done for me and the amazing friendship you've offered. Your support truly means so much!

Photographer Wander Aguiar and team - Thank you so much for the amazing support you've been kind enough to show Jamie and I. We look forward to many future collaborations and fun times.

Formatter Brenda Wright – Thank you for making my work look professional and beautiful. I truly appreciate it and the kindness you've shown me. I look forward to working with you many times in the future, and, hopefully, one day tasting one of those delicious cupcakes you're always posting photos of!

My Blogger Friends –YOU ARE AMAZING! I LOVE YOU! No really, I do!!! You take a new chance on me with each book, and, in return, share my passion with the world. You never truly get enough credit, and I'm forever grateful!

My Readers – I love you. You make my life possible, thank you. I can't wait to meet many of you this year and in the future!

Table of Contents

COMMON MC TERMS

MC - Motorcycle Club

Prez - President

VP - Vice President

SAA - Sgt. at Arms

Ol' Lady - Significant Other

Chapel - Place Where Church is Held

Clubhouse/ Compound – MC home base

Church - MC 'Meeting'

Original Oath Keepers MC:

Prez – President

Ares – Enforcer, SAA

Cain – Club Brawler

2 Piece – Gun Runner

Twist – Unholy One, Clean up

Spin – Treasurer

Snake – Prospect

Smiles – Road Captain

Shooter – Prospect

Relinquish

Scratch – Prospect

Relinquish: (verb)

Give up, surrender, release, yield, abnegate, cede, resign, forgo.

DEDICATED TO:

My grandmother, without her

I wouldn't be the person I am today.

2 Piece

Church...

"Brothers!" Prez booms out and peers around the table. "It seems we have a reptile problem. Apparently, my son, Brently, hooked up with some female named Seraphina. Guess this bitch is the sister to a brother in the Twisted Snakes MC. Once this clown found out who my son is, he started giving him shit about me. Now, not only are they harassing Brently, but they're trying to sell in our fuckin' territory. Y'all know what happened to the last little roach that tried selling in our territory."

Everyone nods and replies, "Yes."

"Cain, call up the Russian; see if he has dealings with them and what you can find out. It'd be nice if this could be handled easily and we don't have to kill anyone this time," he growls, irritated.

"Sure, Prez, no problem," Cain replies, and Prez waves his hand to the side.

Cain gets up to go make that phone call. When Prez tells you something at the table and waves toward the door, it means ASAP, no fucking around.

Ever since Tate found out what was happening when we were in Tennessee, he's been in charge of the Russian Mafia back there. I'm not sure what happened to his father, Gizya. Knowing the Mafia though, I'd say he's floating in one of the many lakes around Knoxville. That is unless Tate and Viktor decided to show him some mercy and let him leave the business with his tail between his legs.

Sneaky old bastard tried to get the club hooked on his fucking drugs. If we were that spun out on drugs all the time, Prez would kick our asses out. We try to keep that kind of thing out of our area. The less of that shit around, then the fewer problems we have to deal with close to the club.

"Besides that, it's business as usual, brothers. Stay out of jail, party, and enjoy the pussy." He slams the gavel down and we are dismissed.

Our church is always short and straight to the point. Prez tells us to enjoy the pussy, but he rarely partakes in that luxury himself.

I'm not so much of a saint however. My dicks on a schedule and the club whores all know it. I'm not ashamed of the fact I'm a hoe myself. I've come to terms with it and have embraced it. I don't do any fucking drama, and regular pussy is a must.

Cain's sitting in the usual booth with a bottle of Jack and lemons. Reckon I'll head over to join him. There's nothing like a rich shot of that amber colored liquid after discussing business.

Cain's a newer member to the club, but is fitting in well. He'll probably become an Enforcer with Ares one day. Those two enjoy messing up some fools and fighting whenever they get wound up. We've become close friends since I found his ass out in Cali. Poor kid seemed a little lost.

That Cali trip was chill. I got to visit my younger sister, Sadie. I hadn't seen her in six months. It felt good to catch up with her.

I feel like a shitty older brother letting us drift so far apart. We've always been close—physically and emotionally. I wish she'd just move around here so I can check on her more. She isn't motivated to go anywhere yet, unfortunately.

I don't understand why she stays; maybe there's a man or something. I didn't see anybody when I was there though and I stayed damn near two weeks. She's my sister and I love her, but fuck is she stubborn.

I learned real young to stay out of her way and let her be independent if she chose to. In the end, if shit didn't go her way, she'd eventually come to me. It worked out for the best like that.

Relinquish

Our home life sucked and we had to adapt quick. Sadie learned to depend on me for a bit of everything at an early age. I enjoyed helping with her when she was a baby; it made me feel like a good brother to get her a bottle of milk or find her a toy to play with. Then my role evolved into being the older sibling who taught her the simple things, like how to tie her shoes and how to catch worms when it rained.

Dad took off on our family after Sadie was born. According to Mom, he didn't want the responsibilities. I don't get how one kid was okay, but two became 'responsibilities.' What the fuck do you call one kid?

I'd enjoy seeing the dick now. I'd give him a piece of my mind after what we went through growing up.

Sadie's always rationalized that he left because she wasn't a boy. She has it in her head he would've stayed. She's crazy; that bastard was going no matter if she was a girl or a boy.

He never visited, called, or sent anything either. Well, he couldn't call after a while because the phone got shut off, along with the cable. Food became slim pickings and if they hadn't owned the house prior to, then the electric and water would've been shut off as well. They did get shut off, eventually.

Mom, she was just vacant. Once Dad took off, she quit caring. If it wasn't for Dad's disability checks, we never would've made it as much as we did.

I can still imagine Sadie running around with her blonde pigtails and wearing my hand-me-down T-shirts. She was such a pretty little girl growing up, but drowned in my clothes that were far too big for her. We were poor, so we didn't have a choice. Hell, we didn't know any different.

I didn't realize it back then, but I'd always made sure she had snacks out to eat and her room was cleaned up. I was a neat freak, so I guess I did it out of habit. I liked everything in a certain place, so it came natural to fix things in the house that got messed up.

Sadie grew bigger and I became more protective of her. I sat with her on the bus each day and walked her to her class. Then I'd meet her at the end of the school day and walk her to our bus to come back home.

I'd help her with her homework and teach her everything school related that I knew. She picked up on stuff quickly and did well with her grades. I was always a proud brother having her show me her report card when she brought it home. I'd already done the same schoolwork myself, so it was easy for me.

The first time I knew things were changing, I was fourteen. I attempted to cook Sadie a grilled cheese sandwich after school and the stove wouldn't work. I freaked out, thinking I'd broken it. Nope, that dumb bitch hadn't paid the bills. She'd been doing it more and more frequently, skipping payments.

That's when shit started to get worse. I found out she was doing heroin. We were dirt poor, and mix in heroin, there's no room for anything else. I became angry inside, worrying for my sister's safety and how we were supposed eat every day.

I started to pick up any odd jobs I could find, to help as much as possible. The old Ace Hardware store owner knew me from stopping by and trying to learn how to fix things myself, since we could never hire anyone. He eventually gave me a job and it helped me pay for food and the utilities. I mowed lawns and picked weeds when I had free time.

Once Sadie was old enough to work, she started helping at Ace on the weekends during the busy hours. Thankfully it gave her enough money for the things she'd needed. I was a young boy, how was I supposed to know girls needed more shit than boys did?

She hit twelve years old and I had no clue what to do with her. I knew if a boy looked at her funny though, he'd get his ass beat. If a girl was malicious towards Sadie at school, I'd spread a rumor that she was a whore. Eventually people caught on and Sadie had a pretty decent time in school.

Things didn't get much easier from there on out. It was difficult to try and work, plus finish high school. Sadie wasn't going to quit, no matter how hard I had to struggle. I made a pact with myself when I found Mom doing drugs. I wouldn't let Sadie go down that same path.

When I was seventeen, Mom split as well. She'd needed a fix so bad that she started breaking shit and tearing the house apart. She came at me with a knife, and I'd told her to get the fuck out. I'd kill her before I let her put us through more shit.

I didn't ask for this life, and neither did Sadie. We didn't deserve the hand we were dealt, we made it work though. We fought and struggled, but I'd be goddamned if I let my sister sink and pay the price for our parents' stupidity.

Once Sadie graduated and could work as a receptionist for a local doctor, I was finally able to live my life a bit. Moving away from her was hell for a while. Not only was I her older brother, but I watched out for her as a quasi-parent, too. I had to move though. I needed to get away from the constant reminder of what life was like growing up.

Sadie believes one day Mom or Dad will return to the house. I pray for her sake, it never happens. I changed all the locks and eventually made sure the windows were replaced as well. I figured it would at least help keep them out, if one of them were to ever show up.

I stop by and visit her whenever I have a run up in that part of the country. I need my freedom now that she's grown. I guess you can call it making up for lost time or some shit. I don't like to feel any strings attached, holding me down, besides my sister.

Joining the club was a tough-enough decision for me. I wasn't sure I could handle more roots until I got to know them well.

I was about to head back home to Texas when I'd run into Cain. He was on his piece-of-shit bike. I could tell when I first saw him he'd had a rough life, same as me.

The club has a lot of stragglers, so I knew he'd be welcomed. Most of the members had rough lives growing up as well. We've all dealt with some dark shit at some point in our lives, and some of us still fight with it.

I count myself lucky; all I dealt with growing up was missing parents. I'm still fucking jaded though. I'll probably never have children of my own. I had to grow up too fast.

It's all good though; I got Sadie out of the whole mess and she's worth it. I may not give a shit about my own life, but I'll always be proud of my little sister.

I love going on runs all over the country too, not just Cali. It's like I can hop on my bike and ride away from any problems I may have. You also never know what you may find or who you may meet — like Cain, for example.

He was lost and now he's found. It's an awesome feeling knowing that I've helped him find his way. He's happy and has a wonderful life with his ol' lady and kid now.

There's nothing in the world like the feeling of freedom I get, riding my bike down a long, open stretch of highway — the wind whipping against you and some good tunes to listen to — it's just you and your bike. It's refreshing and relaxing, my own piece of bliss. Speaking of that, I can't wait to head back to Tennessee. Hopefully I'll get to make a trip soon. There's a certain sexy brunette I plan to hit up again. It's been months since I last had her in my bed and I can still remember every dip and angle of her smooth body.

"2," Cain greets, as I sit across from him in the navy-blue booth. I set my rocks glass down in front of me and chin lift toward it. "Too fuckin' lazy to pour your own shots now, huh, brother?"

This little prick is always giving me shit about my age. I'm barely a few years older than him and still look better than him. He's lucky his ass ain't a prospect any more, or else I'd make him scrub a fucking toilet or two just to fuck with him.

"You jealous fucker, I'm only a few years older. Quit your bellyaching and pour me some Jack," I grin. "You been talking to that bike of yours again?" I rib, good-naturedly.

I may be a touch older but I'm also in my prime right now. I look the best I ever have, feel fan-fucking-tastic, and I'm ready to face shit head on.

"Ha, motherfucker. I heard you talking to yours the other day, too," he snickers, and I chuckle.

This man is obsessed with that custom 883 of his. We all enjoy hassling him about it, too. It's a sweet bike; the brothers and I think it's pretty sick. I personally favor my Hog; she's my baby—all glossy black and chrome. It's a bitch polishing that chrome up, but I don't mind.

"Nah, man, it's cool. How's London and Jamison doing? I haven't seen her around much." Brother seems happy so I don't think anything's up.

"They're good, thanks for asking. Jamison's walking around the house, getting into shit like he owns the joint. He keeps sweet cheeks busy. I'm just trying to knock her up again." He flashes a wicked grin.

"You're nuts, bro; you're going to have like twenty kids in all of five years. You're going to be living here at the club, just to stay sane."

I'm glad the brother has found something to look forward to. He and London are going to be a couple that stays together forever. They have that real happily-ever-after shit going for them and are pretty much obsessed with each other. I hope Cain realizes how lucky he is to have what most of us want, deep down. We just pretend like we don't, and fuck as many club sluts as it takes to hide that emptiness.

Sure, there're a few brothers who want to remain single, just to have a good time. There're also plenty of brothers discreetly looking for their 'ride-or-die' chick. I'm in the middle — on the fence — about it.

I figure it's either gonna' happen when it's time or it won't. There isn't shit I can do about it and I'm not about to substitute it with the first thing that wags her ass in front of me.

"Nah. I love her being knocked up with my kid in her belly. She's so goddamn gorgeous and eats good shit. Now, she's eating healthy and bitching that her hips have gotten wider. I keep telling her it's because her body was created to have my babies. I love that chick. Best fucking thing we ever did was go to Tennessee."

I nod and sip my whiskey.

He may be crazy wanting a car load of kids, but at least he enjoys aged whiskey and loves his woman fiercely. I wasn't sure for a while. She took off and Cain moped around like a drunken ghost.

I hope one day I can find me a good woman like London. Once they came back here and Cain bought her that house, it's like she completely embraced our life. She's smart, beautiful, and respectful of the club. She could be the poster child for an ol' lady.

I guess she's a firecracker at home though. Cain's always talking about her stirring shit up with him so they can have makeup sex and role play.

"Yeah, been thinking about that too," I admit and shrug.

"You mean you've been thinking about Avery." He tips his cup towards me wearing a sly smirk.

Of course, I've been thinking about Avery. She's the best piece of pussy I've ever had; she hugs my dick like a tight fist.

She's visited twice since London came back. It's only been for a few days at a time though. Each visit, she hangs with London during the daytime and then stays the night here with me. I thought she might freak at first about the club, but she didn't care. We always stay holed up in my room anyhow, so she's only met a couple of the brothers.

"Maybe," I shrug nonchalantly. I don't like people all up in my shit. I know Cain will be all over that shit like a bitch in heat if he gets wind of me missing her.

"Maybe my ass, just text her. She talks about you every time London speaks to her on the phone. I know she wonders what you're up to and if you're ever heading to see her."

I shake my head. "I'm good. I'll catch up with her the next time she visits, same as last time she was here."

God, the last time, it was fucking bliss, having her around. We had so much fun together. I love it that she's so forward with me and free-spirited. She belongs on a bike exploring the country. She can also make a mean cup of coffee and that shit matters a lot the morning after you've been fucking all night.

"Anyhow, did you get ahold of that Russian friend of yours?"

Tate's not so bad for overseeing the Mafia in America. He stays calm and collected no matter what. When we went to Tennessee, some bad shit popped off with his best friend.

The man didn't even blink when he had to order the hit on Cameron. The fool had lived with him and everything! Tate's the kind of fucker you should fear, but he's also the best type of ally to have in your corner.

"Yeah, I spoke to him. And he ain't my Russian. He's practically my brother-in-law with how close London and Emily are," he gripes and tips his whiskey back to drink it in one swallow, then bites into his lemon.

He's a weird dude, eating lemons with his drink all the time. I scrunch up my nose and shoot him a disgusted look, he just laughs.

"Well, did you talk to Prez about it and what did you find out?" I ask the million-dollar question since he's not offering shit up like a normal person would when talking.

"I told Prez what Tate said as soon as he walked out of church. You were too busy taking a piss and then screwing around behind the bar."

I scoff and cross my arms. "I wasn't screwing around; none of you fucks wash the glasses so I was cleaning my shit to drink out of. Excuse me if I'm trying not to get mono from the nasty ass glasses." He just rolls his eyes and I shoot him an icy glare.

Come on, already. He likes to drag shit out because it gets me going. It always ends up with us trading arm punches and that fucking hurts.

He's the club Brawler so he's always lifting weights and working out. Every time we play arms, I end up with around twenty bruises and can barely lift my limbs the next day. I'm no small man by any means, but he punches fuckers for a living. I'm six-foot-two and I think he has an inch on me and probably about twenty more pounds. I'm lean but muscular, and Cain's just plain solid everywhere.

"All right, geez, Tate said he doesn't have shit to do with the Twisted Snakes, but he's going to ask his brother, Viktor. I guess when Tate took over as Big Boss a few months ago, him and his uncle started talking to Viktor about taking over the Bratva. He thinks the Bratva might have had some dealings with them but he's not one hundred percent sure. He's supposed to call me back tonight. Prez is probably going to call church again when he finds out what Tate says, so be prepared." He finishes and I nod.

"You bouncing?" I pour another shot.

"Yeah, man. I have to get back to the baby momma and all."

I smirk at his baby momma comment. They've been calling each other that shit since she first found out she was pregnant, nearly a year and a half ago. I can't believe it's been that long already, and Jamison is his own little person now.

The dude's cool, too. All the Brothers treat him as their own when London brings him around here.

Only a few members have kids, so I guess that makes us the cool uncles to him. I'm undecided about having kids. I could see the enjoyment of it, but I'm not at that point in my life yet. I want to spend some time with someone for a while before I start planting my seed.

"Cool, tell her what's up for me. Ride safe, Cain."

"Always man, take it easy." He chin-lifts, placing his cup in the bar sink. He shoots me a two-finger salute on his way out the club door.

I sip on my whiskey and savor the burn as it trickles down the back of my throat.

Lucky fucker, going home to his ol' lady.

This life is a great one and you're surrounded by your brothers all the time, but it can still get lonely. I finish up and put my glass in the bar sink as well. I had to wash my own, so these lazy asses can do the same.

Avery

I set yet another college student's coffee down on the counter. I really should stop working in these damn coffee shops. I go from A Sip of Heaven to Brewed. At least Brewed allows me to drink coffee for free as long as I make it, myself.

Relinquish

Woohoo, that is, if I actually was a coffee drinker.

I like it sometimes but not a crazy amount or anything. The other shop made me pay for everything, except faucet water. Their water had a yellowish tint to it too, so that was a serious no-go.

The owner tried to play it off as the Tennessee water system. Yeah, right — water system, my ass. He was full of shit too. I have the same tap water at home and amazingly, mine comes out clear. I'm thinking his pipes are full of rust and he's slowly poisoning the city of Knoxville. It wouldn't surprise me since he's a penny pincher on everything else.

I'm so sick of being here. I'm almost finished with school though. These accounting classes are so boring; I could watch paint dry and get more of a show.

One more semester of summer college life, then it's off to the big world. I'm going to school for accounting; Mom and Dad say it's a real job. Truth is, I don't know what I'll do with my degree. It's terrifying to think of.

I could attempt to get a job at an accounting firm. Who knows if they'd even call me for a damn interview though. No matter how much I try, I just can't imagine my life sitting behind a cubicle or in a box-sized office. That doesn't sound fun or life fulfilling at all, some may enjoy it and more power to them.

This growing up crap has me thinking about my age too. Getting older is for the birds. I miss my biggest worry of eating cereal and watching cartoons on Saturdays.

I can't believe I'm twenty-three years old. God, when did that happen? It seems like I just blinked from being twenty-one. Now *that* was a fun age for me. It's amazing I didn't end up needing to have my stomach pumped from hitting the fraternity parties so much. Those were some good times.

A scorching-hot burning sensation comes over me and I gasp. It's like my hand is touching a stove burner lit up with a hot flame. I glance down quickly. "Shit!" I shriek and drop the metal milk steamer thingy.

Damn it.

I'm forever getting burned by these stupid coffee machines. Well, in this case, the container that you use to steam milk in. What happened to an old-fashioned cup of coffee? I mean if you like sweet, just add a shit ton of sugar to it and voila! Done!

I shake my hand crazily beside me and bring my fingers to my lips, hoping my saliva will cool the burn. It doesn't work; it only makes it hurt worse. I yank my fingers out next and blow on them hard.

I end up flailing my hand around maniacally like I'm an injured bird or something. *Fuck, that hurts, bastard devil coffee machine!* These things could be torture devices if someone were creative enough.

"You all right, sweetie?" Dillan peers at me, worried.

She's always kind and compassionate when she witnesses one of my accidental injuries. The girl is gorgeous too with bright red hair and perfectly tanned skin. She has a diamond Monroe piercing that makes her look super-hot. I'm not against kissing a chick, and her I'd kiss.

I really like Dillan a lot. Some people you have to work with are total dicks and slackers, but not her. She's always in a decent mood and isn't afraid to help someone out if they need it. I hope I come off as the same. Well, when I'm not busy burning myself and yelling at coffee machines.

"Yes, ma'am, I am. Thanks for asking. You mind finishing his order so I can clean up though?" I wheeze, shooting her a defeated look.

I'm so over this day. I need like a year-long vacation to an island, with lots of rum. Or Vodka, Tequila — whatever. I'm not picky. Oh, and a bottle of sunscreen; yup, sounds perfect.

"Yeah, hun, go ahead. Why don't you just take your break now too and have a cuppa."

I nod and make my way to the closet-sized break room. The last thing I want right now is a cuppa. I want a freaking strawberry lemonade and they only have those at Sonic. I take in the room; checking over the rack we hang our crap on and the tiny, desk-sized table with a plastic chair.

The lights dim and the walls are dreary beige. *Fantastic.* It's so boring in here I could take a nap.

I grab a clean apron off one of the hooks on the walls.

God, I have to get out of here. I'm so sick of the everyday responsibilities and routine. All this work and for what? For bullshit, that's what.

Ugh, who am I kidding? I'm probably never leaving this shithole. I'll end up being a barista for the rest of my life and let my accounting degree go to shit. Or maybe I'll be lucky enough to find a few people who need me to do their taxes on the weekends.

My phone alerts me to a text message. I quickly snatch it out of my pocket, ignoring the stinging ache radiating throughout my palm.

Niko: A! You want to party tonight?

It's just my buddy, Nikoli. That's the extent of our relationship now, partying and buddies. We were friends with benefits for a while. He was decent in the sack, too.

Not to mention he's also damn good looking at like six-foot-five and covered in tribal tattoos. He has blond hair and strong Russian features. I always tease him with the line from Rocky, 'I must break you.' He watched the movie just because I kept teasing him. He says it's crap, that he looks nothing like him.

Right. That man is built just like him. Niko is straight eye candy for your girly parts and the Tennessee chicks here eat that shit up like crazy. Throw in the accent and the bitches are done for.

We're much better as friends it turns out; we're too much alike. It got to the point where it was like sleeping with

31

my brother. Well, if I had a brother, that's what I imagine it would be like. But I never imagined my brother being hot. So anyway, it just became awkward.

When London started porking Cameron, I began seeing Niko. I got away from Cameron as quickly as possible. That controlling shit he tried to pull all the time was not for me.

Sometimes I'll look for him at school, but I'm guessing he graduated. He's not living at Tate's anymore either. Niko moved into Tate's house full-time now. It's like Cameron just up and disappeared one day.

I asked the guys, but they both said he'd left the country. To just up and leave and not contact anyone, seems strange to me. Especially since he was best friends with Tate and Niko, but it's whatever. No skin off my back.

Do I want to party with Niko tonight? Hmm, no. I'm not in the mood like I usually am. Guess I'm going to be a shitty wingman tonight and not help him get laid.

Me: Nope getting fat from Snickers ice cream. You're welcome to join me.

Niko: No way José! I'm going to bar.

I burst out laughing. It's pretty freaking funny to see a Russian using 'José' in a sentence. Any kind of silly line or shirt Niko finds, he incorporates into his speech and wardrobe.

It's even more comical since he's this monster-sized bodyguard to the Russian Mafia Boss. I wouldn't change him for the world though. Some days he's my sunshine on a cloudy day.

I bought him a T-shirt for his birthday that says BEEF in big bold letters across his chest and has a picture of a slice of cake underneath. He loved it and put it on right away. I thought it was hysterical and great all at the same time.

Me: Your loss, taco.

Niko: Taco? That has nothing to do with ice cream. If you make food, I come.

Me: LOL, never mind. I'm eating ice cream. You have fun, and stop by if you get bored.

Niko: K. Later gator.

Me: After while crocodile ☺

Niko: O, I like that one.

I giggle some more. I love his Russian language and accent. It's beautiful and makes him sound sillier sometimes. He even texts like he would say it. I'm not messaging him back. Once you get him started, he can go all day.

I wonder what Emily's up to. I miss my bestie. Ever since she found out she was pregnant a few months ago, Tate's been following her around like he's wearing a leash. Who knew a little baby could turn hard-asses into mush.

Same goes for Cain. He's had baby fever since I first met him. He and London have the cutest little boy that I've ever seen.

I know Tate and Emily will be the same way. I'm excited for them all. I just don't have the same desires right now. I want to have fun and live as much as possible, save the growing up for later. I'm trying to only drink bottled water just in case pregnant dust is in the water or something. Screw that!

I guess I'd have to have sex first. Normally, that wouldn't be an issue for me. I really enjoy the male anatomy. Ever since the last time I saw 2 Piece though, no one has made it past my front door. They just don't compare to him at all in any department.

I keep asking London if they're planning a trip to visit anytime soon. Hopefully, with Emily pregnant, they will. Tate and Emily always go to Texas. I know Emily likes to check on her grandfather's house and visit London's family too.

If they visit here, then 2 Piece will ride up with them in case they run into any shit. Cain's funny about being protective when it comes to London and the baby. I'm guessing he's paranoid something will happen since he's a biker.

It just sucks because each time Tate and Emily make a trip, if I can't get enough time off, then I can't go with them. I've only been able to go on two of the six trips they've taken.

I can't afford to drive down there by myself or I would. I barely squeeze by as it is on my wages.

I was going to work at one of Tate's businesses, but I couldn't. If I decide to up and quit or something, I don't want it to damage our friendship in any way. It'd be stupid to piss off the Mafia, even if he swears they aren't after me. There's always that inkling of doubt in the back of my head that they aren't as sweet as they appear to be.

I'd hope that with my friendship to Niko and Emily, they'd at least try to save my butt. Who knows though? I just figure out my own way to make it.

I head out of the break room back to the front counter. I'm sure my break is way over by now. I'm a little bad about timing; I end up running late or early often.

"Feeling better, hun?" I look up as Dillan approaches and nod.

"Yes, thanks. Sometimes I become a tad overwhelmed. Sorry about that and thanks for taking over."

I give her a side hug and a small smile. The boss would probably write me up if he were here to see me freak out like I did. Good thing it's usually just the two of us in the evenings.

"Of course, lady, I don't mind at all. I was coming to let you know that I filled Justin in on how dead the place is. He said we can close up thirty minutes early, so start your side work." She jumps up and down, clapping her hands a few times, making me grin. Thank God there are only a few cameras or we'd look like a couple of fruit loops.

One positive thing about working in a coffee shop near campus is that we get to close in the evenings instead of super late like I've seen some coffee houses do. Everyone's usually out with friends, partying or doing homework. Plus, I'm sure for safety reasons, it's smarter to just close up shop.

"You're freaking awesome, thank you." I cheer and blow her a kiss.

She catches it dramatically and brings her hand to her chest. Making me giggle and turn up the store radio. "Sex on Fire" by Kings of Leon begins to play and we both dance around, singing while we clean.

I know I'm not a kid, but I love to have fun and act silly. My life would be much more boring if I never did anything like this.

I pretend to play the air guitar and she pretends to play drums. Dillan totally has a thing for drummers. I don't blame her with that Hawk guy at Tainted. He's über hotness with his blue mohawk and muscular drummer arms. They'd make an adorable couple too with Dillan's model-like features and wild, red hair.

After finishing up the shift duties as quickly and efficiently as possible, we both hightail it out of there. I plan to go home and eat copious amounts of my favorite ice cream that Emily and London got me hooked on. Damn heifers, I now own every sundae topping imaginable too.

Dillan takes off to get her own food and probably pick Hawk up something, per her usual. What is it about men and food? If it's not sex they want, then they seem to be hungry.

2 Piece

Called into Church again...

I'm guessing Prez and Cain must've discovered some shit, since Prez called us into church again. It's not our usual meeting time or day.

I take my seat three spaces down from Prez. It goes in pecking order, and while I'm slowly making my way up, there are still a few people ahead of me. It's a good thing, though. I don't want to oversee all the club shit—too much of a hassle.

Prez slams the gavel three times. Everyone shuts up and gives him their full attention.

"Listen up," he grumbles.

I take in his scruffy, tired face. He's stressed about something that's for sure. Every time he gets worked up he doesn't sleep.

He rubs his left hand over his face in irritation and sighs loudly. "We got word from the Russians. They know about the fucking Snakes but aren't supplying them with anything. It looks as if they get their shit from Mexico. Who has any contacts with the Mexican cartels?"

He glances around the table and we all remain quiet. "Fuck, nobody? This day just keeps getting better." He shakes his head and stares down at the table in front of him for a second.

He glances back up, frustration clearly written across his face. "Well, boys, then I have no choice. I'm gonna' have to call Tate back and let him send up his man that he offered."

Chaos breaks out with the brothers. Many start complaining and Twist hits the table with his fist angrily. With all of us in here, it tends to get a little crowded. With several griping comments such as 'bullshit' amongst other protests, the noise lever raises rapidly.

"The fuck's this about?" Smiles jumps in.

Prez shoots his chilling glare at him and snarls. Nobody yells at the table except Prez. It's the only time he demands we show him the respect of his patch.

Prez leans over the table and slams his palm down, directly in front of Smiles. There's an audible growl, but I'm not sure who it comes from. They stare each other down for at least a minute, if not longer. It's like watching two savage animals about to rip each other apart.

Prez blinks then shakes his head and sits back in his chair. There's always been a rift between the two of them. I heard Smiles was keen on Prez's ex ol' lady.

I'm surprised the fucker's alive still, if that really was the case. "Just calm the fuck down, everybody. Tate offered to send up his right-hand man, Niko. They want this problem to disappear as much as we do. Trust me when I say we don't want the cartels into our shit. I'm going to tell Brently to stick close to the club till we have this figured out. Right now, it's just a Snake problem. I want it to stay that way so we can take care of it."

Twist shakes his head appearing disgusted; his lip piercing glints off the sunlight shining through the window as he does. He taps his fingers quickly in a beat, almost compulsively. An evil smirk comes over his face. "Just send me to check 'em out, Prez. I can be an exterminator if needed."

Prez shakes his head and shoots Twist a look that says, 'shut the fuck up, you're trying my patience,' then glances at each of us around the large table. "We don't act this way; we get pissed, but we think about shit. Now I know y'all don't want any kind of help around here. If it comes to them saving your lives though, I'm doing what's best for my brothers. You put me here to take care of the Oath Keepers MC and its members. That's exactly what I'm doing."

He takes a drink of his bottled water and clears his throat. "Now in the interest of this club's survival and protecting my family from a possible threat, we will have a visitor. No bullshitting and no fucking around. Y'all treat him with respect while he's here and always. They've been nothing but helpful to us. Understood?"

The table spits out, "Yes, Prez," in a chorus of irritated voices. We sound like a bunch of petulant teenagers who just got grounded to their rooms for the summer.

"Anything else we need to be discussing?"

I blink, sit up and nod to acknowledge I want to speak when he looks at me. "Uh, yeah, I was thinking about asking my sister, Sadie, if she wants to come for a visit. If we're going to catch a lot of heat for this Twisted Snakes shit, then I'll hold off."

Prez shifts in his seat and runs his hand through his shoulder-length blond hair. "Nah, brother, family is always welcome. Things aren't too bad yet, so definitely ask her. I'm sure the brothers would enjoy some fresh meat round here," he chuckles.

I glower at him. "Fuck no! None of you fuckers even talk to my sister if she visits." I warn, good-naturedly and everyone chuckles.

That's one of the first things that drew me to the club life: the sense of loyalty and devotion that the brothers show toward their family members and each other. Here at the club, I never feel like I'm struggling or fighting alone, like I did growing up. When I was younger, I was in a constant state of feeling as if I was drowning and wasn't going to be saved.

The club stepped in and threw me that life preserver I so desperately craved. I'm completely grateful that I always have someone near to help me out with anything if need be. I got a little taste of the generosity and loyalty of the club the very first time I rode to Texas, many years ago.

I'd just crossed into west Texas near Abilene and my bike began making crazy noises. I wasn't a real mechanic or anything and had no idea what to do. I tinkered with shit and half-assed fixed stuff my whole life, but I was at a loss. I had to pull over; I didn't want it to completely break or I knew I'd never be able to repair it.

An hour or so later, Prez and some of his members rode up. I about shit my pants, being confronted by a group of mean looking fuckers. At the time, I was a lot younger and smaller in size.

I thought they were going to rob me and possibly kill me. I had no clue just how ignorant I really was. I guess now though, I see many others are just as unfamiliar to our ways.

Imagine my surprise when the brothers gave me a bottle of water, helped me fix my bike, and let me ride with them to a truck stop down the road for a burger. They wanted to make sure my bike didn't fuck up again after they took off. They turned out to be a decent bunch of rough guys.

The Prez was kind and easygoing towards me immediately and I got a sample of the life I could have. I was hooked from then on, but still leery for a bit about the commitment they'd devoted to the club. Over time, they grew into the family I never really had, minus my sister.

I've always wanted Sadie to come down and be a part of things here. She deserves to have a family supporting her and be surrounded by people who'd care about her. I think she'd end up enjoying it as much as I do. I've always loved club life and dedicated a lot of my time to it.

"All right, on that note, this shit's done." Prez states and the gavel's slammed once to signify the ending of church.

We all slide our chairs back and head to the bar. I know there will be a lot of bitching and moaning over Nikoli coming up. I personally don't mind Niko. I get a good vibe from him. He seems like he's dedicated to Tate and taking care of shit. I can usually tell if a fucker's shady.

The hall's dark as I make my way towards the bar. On the walls, there's a banner with our club crest and a few pictures scattered about of the clubhouse being built. We celebrated the club's resurrection with a large barbecue outside all day and drank plentifully into the night. That was before we had club issues to deal with and we were just a group of guys riding.

The club's been around a lot longer than I've been in it. The compound however, is only about five years old. We're a cluster of wanderers who are all native-by-choice Texans. We love our state, never met a group of more proud people. I love traveling around the US, but there's something about southern air that just pulls me more towards it.

Grabbing the first clean glass I find, I head over to Cain and Ares' booth. These two have been getting cozy with each other, but I'm still close with them both regardless of their own budding friendship.

"'Sup, brother." I meet Ares' gaze. He's a big man; the type you'd believe could bench-press his bike for shits and giggles.

I throw a chin nod at Cain and Ares gestures for me to sit.

"Brother." Cain gives me a two-finger salute as I pull up a chair, plopping my glass on the table.

It lands with a loud *thunk* and he smirks, "That serious, huh?" Ares grin's teasing.

I had to go on a few runs with him when I was newer to the club. Our Prez likes for the Enforcer to sort of break people in. He took me to shake some fools down. It got a little bloody but I handled it.

Since then, we've been cool with each other. I wouldn't ever want to go again though. I don't have a strong stomach for some of that shit and try to save it for the times it's really called for.

"I'm good man, hook a brutha' up," I answer with a smirk, sliding my glass forward with my finger.

Cain tries to hand me a lemon as well, wearing a cheesy smile. His dimples out on display.

"I don't want this shit!" I huff, chuckling and throw the lemon wedge at him. He and Ares both laugh.

Badass MC Enforcers and they fuck around like a couple of kids. I take a long pull of the aged whiskey from my glass and smack my lips in approval.

Exactly what I needed.

"Now that's some good shit. So, you two going to share what the plan is with Nikoli?" I glance at them.

They exchange a look and Ares shuffles his glass, trading it from one hand to the other. He meets my curious stare as his fingers play with the scruff on his chin. "Well, looks like Prez is calling Tate to give him the okay. From my understanding, Niko's going to head up here so he can speak directly to Tate whenever needed. If we require reinforcements or anything, then he can just call for backup. Granted, Tennessee's far away, but they'd be able to make it here in half a day if shit hit the fan. Niko will stay at a hotel in town, but can chill out at the club too. Tate's going to see if he can get ahold of anybody with the cartel to get the gun situation handled on their part. Right now, we're mostly worried about getting Brently close enough to the club so he stops getting harassed." He takes a sip of his drink, and then continues. "I guess the crazy fucks keep leaving dead cats on his apartment doorstep. Not just dead, but slain, with their guts in full view. Those pussies are threatening to gut him. I wouldn't mind having some fun with them myself."

I nod. What a bunch of stupid asses, messing with an MC's President's kid. They should know better, belonging to a club themselves. I guess they'll just have to learn the hard way.

Cain grunts and rolls his eyes. "Why doesn't he just send you, Twist, and me to go teach them a lesson? That'll get shit fixed real quick."

Ares shakes his head, shooting him a chastising look. I think if Cain could solve everything that pisses him off with a fist fight, then he would.

"I already told you, brother; it'll stir up more shit. Listen to Prez's orders. Just chill and wait for them to make their next move. Trust in him, he knows what he's talking about. Quit being an impatient fucker. You don't want to end up dead, when you have London and your kid." Ares appears more like a giant ogre, but the dude is hella' smart.

Cain huffs, crossing his arms, and sits back to basically pout.

Jesus, this is going to turn into a giant shit show. I gesture to Cain to grabbing his attention. "I agree. I'd like to fuck them up, too. I got two pieces in my holster with the Twisted Snake's name on them. I just don't want this shit to come to the compound. How far away does Brently live, anyhow? A couple of hours, right?"

Cain shrugs and takes a long pull of his beer, but Ares nods. "Yeah, brother. I don't think it'll get out of hand enough to come to the clubhouse."

"Good, we'll just make sure to keep it contained. If Sadie comes down, I know she'll be fine." I nod and scoot my chair back. It's time for me to get the fuck out of here. "Well I'm out, y'all enjoy," I mutter as I stand up. Time for me to hit it, then quit it.

They watch me, and Cain stands up. "Later, brother," he fist bumps me. I nod to him and then to Ares.

Avery

I step over to the kitchen table and set Niko's coffee down in front of him. He eagerly reaches for it and beams at the warm refreshment. He has a fondness for my coffee and relishes in the fact that I make it for him exclusively when he comes around.

He has on a plain white T-shirt and jeans today and it catches me a bit off guard. It's strange seeing him appear so casual when he's supposed to be working. I shoot him a befuddled look.

I guess Tate doesn't really care what Niko wears. However, he's always dressed to look professional. Well, unless we have plans to swim or something. He was just explaining to me that Tate wants him to go out of town to handle an issue for a while. I'm assuming that's the reason for the impromptu visit and lack of style in his wardrobe today.

"So, what do you mean you have to go out of town? Is that why you look so plain today?" I gesture towards his chest.

Emily's busy with Tate, London moved to Texas, and now, Niko is taking off too. I seriously don't know why I stay here. Well, besides school. *Oh yeah, because I'm too poor to take my ass anywhere else. Duh.*

"It is exactly as I said. Tate needs me to go check out a few things, so I will be in Texas for a while. Leave my shirt alone, you are still in pajamas."

Wait a minute...did he just mention that he'd be in Texas for a while? *Texas = 2 Piece.* I want to visit Texas, and if Niko's going, then maybe I can tag along.

He's getting so much better with his accent. I can understand nearly everything he says the first time around. In the beginning, he had to repeat nearly everything he'd say at least a few times so we could understand it. Tate hides his accent well, but with Niko it's like a shining beacon.

I wish I had an accent. If I did, I'd never shut up.

I wonder if my parents would lend me some money to take with me. I'll have to call them. I don't normally request to borrow any money or ask for much, so hopefully they won't mind. My dad is constantly enquiring if I need anything, but I'm determined to make it on my own. I know if I accept stuff, then my mom will continuously remind me about it and take the liberty of inserting her nose more into my business.

She was a psycho when I first got my Facebook account and she found me on there. She literally commented on every single post I made. Then she went and friended each person on my friends list. That's pretty much stage one clinger status at that point.

My parents don't have much money, but they have some. It's not like they ever do anything to spend it. I'm sure right now they're busy bumming it at the beach. It must be nice. I work my ass off all the time at jobs and at school, while they just float along through life, not giving a shit. I grew up in Florida and when I was still there they practically lived in the sand and sun.

I love it there, just wasn't too impressed with the colleges. UT had so many cool things to offer someone looking for a new life. Here, I get to branch out on my own and not worry about my parents butting into everything. My mom and dad are the hippy, free-spirit types but also super nosey when it comes to their daughter. You can only tell a person to stay out of your stuff so many times, until you up and move to another state.

I grew up closer to my father. My pops has short, brown hair and he's going bald. However if you mention it, he'll tell you that he just had a haircut.

He's always wearing a smile and it's one of my favorite things about him. Dad's a very intelligent man and has a passive personality. He just goes with the flow and follows Mom around like a devoted puppy, nodding at whatever she says. Personally, I think she drove him crazy a long time ago and gave in, submitting to her dominant persona.

My mother leans more towards the bitchy side. We butted heads a lot while I was growing up. I'm stubborn and she's tenacious, and it doesn't mix well.

She wanted me to be a doctor or something *vital* like that. I finally got her to back off with me being in accounting. I guess she believes those kinds of jobs are important.

I believe the jobs that help animals and keep people safe are much more significant. Like the shelter volunteers at animal clinics or the soldiers fighting in the war. Of course, being a doctor is important, but just not *my* kind of important—not my calling. She probably wishes she had a different kid, and I don't blame her. I'll most likely do a whole lot of nothing with my life and I'll live with it, not her.

I'm normally a happy, outgoing person, but I've been in a bit of a funk lately. I don't know why I'm sad or where these emotions have come from. I think it's probably because I'm at a crossroads in my life and I'm not exactly where I want to be right now. I should've gone to school for something I'd enjoy and be happy doing

I'd love to travel the country and help in different situations. Maybe assist when there's some sort of a disaster and they need volunteers or something. That sounds like it'd be a fulfilling job to have.

I know it'd make me appreciate more of what little I do already have. I can't imagine the devastation some people experience, dealing with the different tragedies. Or even the animals, I'd love to help and work with animals.

The world is full of selfish people, just sitting around doing nothing. It'd be a much better place if more people helped out and were kind to one another. That's one good attribute my parents have; they volunteer a lot. When I go home, I volunteer at the oceanography labs and love it. When my parents visit here, they usually have a Habitat for Humanity project or something related to volunteer for.

With me being a poor student living on my barista's wages, if they visit, they have to stay in a hotel. They'll stop over for a short period of time which keeps the visit nice and not too overwhelming. I go back to Florida around once a year for Christmas, the one time they do send me money.

Don't get me wrong, I had a great childhood growing up. I was very fortunate to have them. My parents are just control freaks when it comes to me, probably because I'm their only child and they were so crazy when they were younger. I think that's one reason why I'm so free-spirited now; it backfired on them. My mother tells me to do something, and I automatically venture in the opposite direction.

"*Shit!*" Niko curses loudly in Russian, making me jump. Turning quickly, I scan over his body to check for what could possibly be wrong but he just looks angry. The coffee cup is on the table and he has a hand grasping each of his thighs.

"What? What happened?" I ask, concerned. His pale Russian face is flushed and he's taking deep breaths. He sends me an irritated look.

"This is so hot, why must you make it burn my tongue? Every time, you make great coffee you make it scorching hot. It smells great, I love the flavor, yet you burn my tongue. *Every time.* Why?" He sticks his tongue out and fans it.

I giggle. He gets so worked up. I'm surprised he even spoke that in English. Normally it would have flown out in Russian.

"Come on, Niko, you know I have to help keep things interesting for you." He shakes his head at me and grunts.

He goes to the sink and fills a glass with cold water then drinks it all in three big gulps. *Geez, no wonder he eats burgers so fast. Do you even taste anything at that point though?* I probably shouldn't point out that he looks like an angry tomato right now.

"We are friends, yet I can still spank you," he grumbles seriously and points at me.

I bust out laughing. *Right*, that man has never spanked me no matter how many times we fucked. He's a gentle lover, yet a beast when someone upsets him enough.

"You, my friend, have been around Tate too much. I'm seventy-five percent sure I'm kinkier than your ass and would be the one to spank you first," I admit and wear my cocky smirk proudly.

He grins then chuckles lowly. "So, he rubs off," he shrug, replying sheepishly.

It makes me laugh even more. "Ah no, pretty sure Emily rubs him off now," I sputter.

Niko rolls his eyes and chuckles louder. "Yeah, man, that's what she said!"

It's my turn to roll my eyes at him. He always ends sentences with 'That's what she said.' "Real cute, Niko. All you're missing is a pony shirt."

"No, I have pony shirt," he mutters seriously, and I start rolling in giggles again. I love him. He has no idea how much fun he is. I swear I'm going to pee if he doesn't stop.

"Okay, okay, okay," I take a deep breath then exhale to calm down a bit. "No more giggle fest ninety-nine." I inhale another breath and prepare to talk as fast as possible before Niko can interrupt me. "*SoIreallywanttogotoTexaswithyoureallyreallybad,*" I mumble and gaze at him with my puppy dog eyes.

"What was that just now? You sound like jumbled kitten."

I grin and repeat myself slowly, "I want to go with you to Texas, please. I want to go really, really badly. And, I'll stay out of your way, I promise."

He sighs a bit disgruntled, "No way, José, I'm working. I don't want anything to happen to you if it goes bad," he shakes his head and places his hands on his hips.

"Please, Niko, Please! I'll stay out of your way. Hey, I could maybe even help out a tiny bit, if you needed me to. You never know, you could require my assistance," I nod in an exaggerated *say yes* motion, and then clasp my hands in front of me, begging dramatically.

"Oh my God," he groans and rubs his hand over the back of his neck. He sits back at the table, leaning forward he rests his elbows on his muscular thighs with his fingers rubbing his temples.

I jump in quickly to keep working on persuading him. *He's getting weaker; only a little more and he will give in.*

"Yes, that's it. I can totally help you with anything. And I swear to stay out of your way. Please?" I whine.

It's not my finest moment, but desperate times call for desperate measures. I'll flat out beg if need be. This could be my mini vacation I desperately have to have but can't afford to go on alone. Not only that, but I will get to see London and 2 Piece.

He shakes his head, chewing on the inside of his lip for a second. "Fine, you can tag along. *Only* if you stay out of my business though, *no* poking nose in Niko's stuff. I will be helping Cain's motorcycle club with a problem. You can see London."

I squeal and jump into his lap to hug him. He just made my whole day—hell, my whole week. "Awesome, Thank you! So, um, when exactly do we leave?" I squeeze his neck and the stand back up.

He glances at his silver-colored watch then looks back at me, not in the slightest rush. "In forty-two minutes."

I blink a few times and process what he said.

"Shit...forty minutes. Okay, I'm packing right now then. I need to bring basically everything. Call the shop for me, please Niko. Tell Dillan I'm flying home to Florida for an emergency and I'm sorry. I'll be back as soon as possible," I call out, already jogging for my closet and begin yanking random clothes off hangers.

I throw a handful of shirts and a hoodie on the bed then go through my flimsy plastic drawers to grab shorts, panties, and a few pairs of socks. I turn to pack it all up and some black material catches my eye.

I pivot back slowly and pull the material out to hold it in front of me. *Yep, this dress needs to come too. If we go out anywhere, I'm totally wearing this shit.* It's a short, fitted dress with a flowy bottom that lands mid-thigh on me. It has a hot pink, satin ribbon that runs down one side of it, and it's my favorite dress in the world.

Grabbing my bag up, I dump my school books n the middle of my bedroom floor. Then head for my bathroom, stuffing all of my toiletries into my now empty purple backpack. *Oh, new pink and blue nail polishes? Yep, need them too.* Never know when you might want to paint your toenails.

I zip the bag up and throw it over my shoulder. Next, I snatch my weekender bag from my bed and stuff my clothes in quickly. Once I'm loaded down, I head back to Niko, determined not to make him late.

He smiles and nods when he sees me. "Not bad, *Bean*, but are you going in your pajamas?"

My confident gaze flicks downward, over my attire. .

Fuck! I'm still wearing pajamas.

A sheepish grin overtakes my mouth and I hold up one finger. I twist around and take off running to change, hearing him laugh loudly behind me.

Crazy man has called me *Bean* after coffee beans since I made him his first cup of coffee.

I pull on my daisy duke jean shorts then a black, fitted V-neck style-shirt and make my way to the front door. Niko chuckles, amused and high fives me on my way out. This isn't the first time he's waited on me to change and I get faster with each pass.

"Let's get this road trip started!" I cheer and I climb into his blue Silverado.

I routinely plug my phone in and turn on my playlist. I'm the automatic DJ each time I ride with him. He learned not to touch the radio because I will not hesitate to smack his hand out of the way or titty twist him.

I select "The Rockafeller Skank" by Fatboy Slim and crank the volume up, then buckle my seat belt. Turning to Niko I'm wearing an excited grin on my face and am met with his beaming smile. He starts bopping his head to the beat, happy to not be stuck on this trip alone any more. Only sixteen hours to go until Texas.

2 Piece

I hear some catcalling and peek over at the brothers. They're busy staring out one of the open bay doors of the garage.

Taking a swig of my longneck, I make my way over to them. It's probably a new club slut or something. We'll all fuck her most likely, so not much to get too wound up over.

"Look at dat' ass, man." Smiles appreciates and lets loose a low whistle. He rubs his hands together like he's about to get to touch it or some shit.

"I'll take her off that Russian and keep her busy," Capone comments then smiles wolfishly.

I wonder if Tate showed up for an impromptu visit. If he hears the brothers talk about Emily that way, he'll end up busting someone's damn knees out. Emily's far from a club whore, she's high class ass now that she's in deep with the mafia.

"Nah, anybody tappin' that, it'll be me or 2 Piece, bet." Ares states and, shakes his head at the others.

Gazing out into the parking lot, I discover what they're talking about. Or rather, who they're jonesin' over.

Niko's giant Russian ass is standing next to his truck talking to Cain and beside him is a shorty with light brown hair and an ass those daisy dukes were fucking made for.

Good Lord, it's perfection. I have to say a silent prayer of thanks and then check her booty out again. Ares has it right; one of us will be hitting that, no doubt.

She jumps up and down excited, using her hands as she speaks. Whatever it is, she seems happy to be here. I just want to see her bounce like that from the front.

Might as well get my foot in the door and introduce myself. Just in case she's not Niko's chick and I can get in her panties later. I set my beer down on the concrete and look to the brothers wearing a mischievous grin. They shake their heads at me, grumbling to themselves. They know if I get ahold of her first, their chances all drop significantly. They won't get to test her out until I'm all done and bored with her.

I trek over towards them and Cain glances at me. I give him a small smirk in greeting and he flashes a grin. Fucker probably knows the exact reason why I'm heading over here.

Niko turns toward me and smiles, "2 Piece, how's it going?"

I grin and nod my hello to him. He puts his hand out and we do a classic handshake as a sign of respect since we belong to different affiliations. The Mafia likes to keep everything formal and business like if you aren't a part of their family.

They've dialed it down a few notches with us, since Tate and Cain are close now. I'm glad it's his ass dealing with the Mafia and not mine. I'm not trying to get all wound up with them. People think bikers are crazy; Mafia Bosses can be just as ruthless.

"'Sup man," I reply and the brunette spins to face me. A wide smile spreads across her face and she sprints the few feet between us, coming straight for me.

Holy shit, it's Avery!

I bear down as she jumps into my arms and the brothers start hootin' and hollering behind me. A few send out loud wolf whistles as well.

I probably look like a damn pimp right now. None of them know that I've been with Avery a few times already. I've always kept her to myself whenever she'd visit and very few people have met her before. The only one who knows how much time she and I have spent together is Cain or London. Ares has run into her from time to time when she's sneaked down the hallway in the clubhouse.

She beams up and I can't stop the grin overtaking my own. She's so fucking gorgeous, she makes my breath catch.

"'Sup, Shorty," I rasp. Damn, she's got me worked up a little and I've barely seen her face. Swallowing, I wet my lips, trying to shake off the feelings she gives me.

She watches me do it, then copies and licks her lips. Avery's gaze meets mine briefly before flicking back to my mouth. I love that this bitch is wild for me whenever she's around.

Dipping my head, I nod, silently telling her to go for it. She leans in, our lips meeting and the sensations overtake my body. I've kissed her many times before when we've been together in the past. It seems like my mouth misses hers more each time we're apart.

I wrap my arms tighter around her until she's molded along the front of my frame. In response, she yanks on my hair, hard, kissing me with passion. She nibbles on my top lip, drawing it between her own.

Yanking my head back, I dip back in for a more controlling kiss. Avery likes me to get a little kinky and demanding with her sometimes. My left hand goes under her ass as I grip her thighs tightly. She moans as I flex my fingers against her skin.

Avery gets me so damn hard when I touch her, that I want to lay her down on the hood of the truck to the right of us. My body demands it that I spread her legs, nice and wide, then fuck her hard to make up for the lost time. She pulls away and I kiss down her neck and suck on a few tender spots, relishing in her giggles.

Leisurely, I lift my head away from her throat. My scruff tickles her flesh, as I move until I get close to her ear where I whisper, "I've missed you, Shorty." I glide her frame down my body easily and hold her steady until she gets her bearings.

The apples of her cheeks tint a bit and it causes a few of her adorable freckles pop against the color. She gazes up at me through her eyelashes with her bedroom eyes and I grit my teeth as she softly admits, "I've missed you, too, 2 Piece."

Nikoli places his hand on my shoulder and I glance over at him curiously. "If I knew you were the real reason she wanted to ride along, I would not have made her beg to come with me," he shares jovially and I chuckle.

Avery reaches over, shoving him and he laughs. She glares and if looks could kill, he'd probably be in an icy tundra at the moment. "Shut it, Niko. You don't have to broadcast it!" This time blushes furiously and turns, so her back is to us and we can't see her embarrassed.

I think it's pretty fucking cute though.

"Oh yes, you want broadcast?" he teases, louder and she squeals.

She spins around quickly and yells, "No- Just, no. Don't broadcast, please, Niko."

He belly laughs and she shoots me a bashful look. I just grin and shake my head. She doesn't need to be embarrassed about shit, especially not over wanting to see me. It sounds to me like she was all over the chance to come visit.

My dick throbs as I take her in from top to bottom. Her light auburn colored hair falls past her shoulders in layers and she has sweet, honey brown irises. She's short, about five foot five, and curvy but still slim. She's got some junk in her trunk but not much up top.

It's all good; she can fuck like no tomorrow. I take in her tiny shorts again and my cock throbs for her, confined away. Avery's my type to a T, damn near perfection in my eyes. I'd never admit it to her though.

Ares chin-lifts at Avery, and she gives him a little finger wave with a flirty grin back. He eats that shit up and glances at me, gloating. He wants a piece of her and she just gave him some attention. I don't know if I should be jealous or not, part of me says yes and the other tells me not to be.

She tilts her head a touch, squinting and trying to get a read on me. She knows I need to have some booty frequently or I become grouchy and have stomach aches. My eyebrow shoots up and she shakes her head, shooting me down. "Humph." I grumble and roll my eyes.

Whatever. She'll want it later on, after she gets a few drinks in her. She's a wild one when she has alcohol thrumming through her blood.

Smirking, knowingly that I'll have her tonight at least, I mumble, "I gotta' get back to the garage."

Niko nods and I throw him a salute. Cain chuckles and shakes his head. Fucker knows I was just shot the fuck down and that shit doesn't happen often or basically ever.

Usually the club whores are all over my dick.

They all call me *'the pretty one'*. I ain't fucking pretty, but I'm damn sure better looking than these fools around here.

My hair's nothing special, your average brown color. My man hair is at the point that it could be classified as scruff or beard. Whichever you prefer, anyhow, it's multicolored. Sometimes it looks more blonde at first glance, others a bit red. Regardless, chicks fucking love it.

Then there are my panty droppers. Yep, women dig men with blue eyes. Not just any blue either, they have to change with the lighting. And they also need to damn near sparkle under lights, bitches love my eyes and devilish grin.

"Later." I head towards the garage and catch Cain chuckling to himself.

I have to remember to get him back later. I throw in an extra little swagger for Avery's sake and my brothers in front of me are all beaming. I grin back and they hit me up with fist bumps as I pass them by.

Ares slaps me on my back, gazing me over, "You hittin' that, 2? Bitch looked at you like you were a fucking ice cream cone, brother."

"Nah, man, but I will be later," I divulge confidently and the brothers laugh.

"Maybe I'll see just how dedicated she is to your cock. She might want someone a little manlier," he chortles and I make the jack off gesture in response.

I glance back over to the truck where Avery stands next to Niko and she seems a little lost. She probably thinks she just fucked up, but I'm cool. I'll find her later and remind her why she was so happy to see me in the first place.

Crouching down next to my bike, I check out my intake. I decide now would be the best time to finish fixing my carburetor, it'll keep my mind occupied. I love working on my girl; it's so relaxing. Nine times out of ten, a little grease and time to think will solve almost anything. If not, then drink a cold one and move on.

Two hours later...

My phone vibrates in my pocket. Checking it, I discover there's some random number calling me from out of state. I hit the silence button and head to my room to clean up. I've got grease on my hands, arms, and shirt.

I go to turn the doorknob and hear music escaping from underneath the door. What the hell? I lean in, yep that's music coming from *my* room.

Grabbing one of my pieces out of my holster, I turn the doorknob as silently as possible. Pushing on the door, I slide it open a crack and peak in. Then I gaze around the best I can without sticking my head completely inside. The radio's on, but there's no one in my room.

Tucking my Glock back into my holster, I walk into my room and close the door, flipping the lock. There's a noise loud enough that I swing around quickly, wanting to get the drop on whomever is in here, first. I scan the room—bed with navy blue comforter and light blue pillows, night stand with my bottle water, alarm clock and Harley magazine, dresser with pile of loose change and my radio that is currently on— all the normal shit. Well, normal minus the radio playing "Dead and Bloated" by Stone Temple Pilots.

I keep everything tidy. I don't care for clutter. Extra shit holds you down and makes things messy.

I've always lectured my sister, because she's the opposite. Seems like Sadie keeps everything she gets her damn hands on. Speaking of, her hands are very small, since she's just brushing five feet tall. I love giving her hell and teasing her about having to climb on the counters to reach shit.

I hear another noise and glance up. *Fuck, it's coming from the bathroom.*

I catch the scent of flowery soap and realize the rooms a little steamy. It was warm outside today so I hadn't paid any attention to the warmth in my room. Avery hasn't been here in a while, so it didn't cross my mind about her being here either. She's a damn radio hog too; I should've guessed it was her.

The door swings open the rest of the way and out steps Avery. Her skins bare, glistening with the remaining water droplets she's missed while drying off. Her russet locks are wrapped in a bright blue towel and she's humming the song to herself. I take her in from top to bottom, paying special attention to my favorite parts. Her pretty, peach nipples are upturned toward the ceiling a little, thanks to her small, pert breasts that're summoning me to touch and explore.

I gulp and it's loud. Damn near comical with what she does to my body. This woman could have me all to herself, three hundred sixty-five days a year if she wanted to, yet she has no idea. She's clueless as to what she does to me whenever we get these small visits with each other. I crave her scent, her taste, her sinful mouth.

My eyes follow along, sliding over her lightly tanned skin. Her pussy's bare and tastes delicious. I know, as I've had my mouth there many times before.

Her thighs part and it's just enough space that I can savor the outline of her lips. She's probably wet down there, right this very minute. I clear my throat and glance up at her face.

Her eyes are dilated and she returns my stare, as if she's ready to devour me as well. I make a "come here" motion with my fingers and she obeys, halting about a foot away. She knows to do whatever's instructed when she's in my room and in return, she'll enjoy every minute of it.

Sucking on my pointer finger, I pull it free, wet and reach for her core. I brush over her swollen pussy lips until I get to her opening and then thrust my finger deep inside. She falls forward into my body, grasping onto my biceps as she gasps a silent moan.

I do my best to keep her quiet when we're together because it turns her on something fierce and in the end, makes her even louder. I fucking love when I get her so wound up, she's ready to climb the damn walls. Her pussy contracts with need, confessing the pleasure I'm bringing her.

She's tight, so fucking tight. My cock's hard and throbbing desperately, practically calling out to her clenched pussy. If it doesn't get what it needs, I feel like I may explode or something. *I want her.*

I run my nose softly along her neck, taking a deep breath, smelling her sweet skin.

"Baby, you've been a good girl, hmm?" I mutter and pump my finger inside her a few times. Each time I insert it, her cunt clenches tightly around it, taunting me. Her cheeks and chest flush as she gets more excited and her stomach

68

muscles tense. "I can smell that delicious pussy getting turned on."

"Oh," she groans, softly and I catch part of it with my lips.

"I'm hungry, Shorty, can I eat that pussy?"

"Fuck, yes, eat it." Her irises glow like molten honey and she pants. "There hasn't been anyone since you." She moans while I push deeper inside her, and she nibbles on her bottom lip. I use my free thumb to pull her lip out and lean in to kiss her softly.

No one else since me? That's been months, if that's the case.

I take her mouth and control the kiss. Not hard, but gently, rewarding her for this gift she's giving me. She keeps up with my tongue, easily kissing me back from all the past practice we've had being together.

Pumping my fingers in and out, I catch each and every gasp in my own mouth through our kiss. It's such a fucking turn on to know that I'm the one doing this to her, making her feel this. I pull out and put an extra, using two fingers inside her. I push in hard and she moans loudly. I feel her tight pussy squeeze me again, mocking my dick.

She needs to be fucked and hard, as badly as I need to be the one fucking her. I kiss down her neck again, biting her flesh. She yanks my hair roughly in return to the point I swear each strand might rip out if she pulls any harder.

Slamming my fingers into her again, harder this time, she detonates, squeezing and pulsing while whispering "2" over and over. She comes, her cunt flooding my fingers with her sweet wetness. I pull them out, rubbing her juices all over her tits and hard nipples then lean in and lick them clean, blowing cool air on each pebbled nipple when I finish.

She's so damn hot and has me wound up like no other. Her breathing's quick and deep, matching my own as I take my fill of her. She's turned on and prepared for me to fuck her and boy oh boy am I ready too.

Avery

God, it feels amazing having him this close to me. I don't know what was going on earlier, but he must be over it. I start to peel his cut off, sliding it down each arm then hand it to him once it's off.

Next, I reach for his shirt and he backs up. *Okay, what the fuck now?* This shouldn't be an issue. We've hooked up a few times in the past and he's never been hesitant.

I peer up at him with a mixture of curiosity and frustration. I may have just had a very satisfying orgasm, but I want the real thing as well. He walks to the dresser and sets his cut on top of it.

"So, we doing this or are we going to hang out and braid each other's hair?" I quip a bit snarky and tap my left foot, my eyebrow shooting up in question.

He purses his lips and then nods. "Yeah, Shorty, just be patient for a second."

"Patient? Are you joking right now? You were practically telling me to fuck in the parking lot earlier." With a pout, I roll my eyes.

"And you made me fucking wait too, so now your ass can chill the fuck out for a few."

He pulls his shirt over his head as he walks toward the door. His colorful tattoos stand out beautifully against his lightly tan skin and his muscled flex with each step. He's a cocky fucker.

It appears that he's going somewhere, but who knows. I shoot daggers at him and huff. Oh, so he thinks he can just tell me what to do, I don't think so. I dropped Cameron's ass like a bad habit when we'd briefly dated and he tried getting too bossy with me.

"Chill the fuck out?" I challenge through gritted teeth, ready to spit nails, if he doesn't retract that rude-ass statement. I won't tolerate a man speaking to me so disrespectfully. I don't give a damn if he's a biker or not.

Sticking my chest out, I clench my stomach muscles then prop a hand on my hip and wait. If we're going to have it out over this, I'm at least going to look fucking amazeballs while doing it.

He cracks his door open enough to stick his head through and I burst, not being able to hold it in, "What the fuck? You're leaving now? What are you doing?"

He turns back to me and holds a finger up for me to hold on a second. I feel like going over there and bending it backwards. It'll teach him to get attitude with me after I've traveled sixteen damn hours to see his face.

"Ares." he hollers into the hallway.

Seriously, this better be good. I'm staring at him for a few seconds before he finally backs away from the door a few steps. He faces towards me and Ares steps inside.

Ares checks me out from head to toe, his eyes glancing over every naked piece of me. As he does, his jaw muscles flex with him clenching his teeth as he breathes out of his nose, with heavy breaths. Shit, 2 was just commenting that he could smell me being turned on. I wonder if that's actually true and it's what Ares smells.

Just fucking great. This is slightly mortifying whenever I think over it.

"Dammit! I'm naked over here, genius; throw me your shirt or something."

My arms quickly cover myself as much as possible. It's a lost cause; no matter where I have my hands, something's exposed. I'm not very shy, but this is a little awkward.

Ares is like a freaking gladiator, he's standing solemnly in his jeans, wearing nothing else. He must've been in his room, relaxing. He's shirtless and without socks, wearing only a pair of light wash, relaxed fit jeans. They hug his hips magnificently.

Ares is pure alpha male and he's stunning.. His chest is broad, a few jagged scars decorating his ribs making him appear even more manly. I'm sure there're some wild stories to go with them too.

My eyes find 2 Piece's and he has a cocky smirk on his face. I don't know what that's about, but he better hurry up with a shirt for me because I'm slightly freaking out inside.

"Oh no, Shorty, you told me you wanted to do this, you were ready to get down. So, let's do this." He spreads his hands wide and motions with his hands like *bring it*.

Freaking fuck head is crazy, stirring stuff up with Ares in here.

Ares eyebrows shoot up, surprised as a bright smile overtakes his face towards 2 Piece.

Holy shit balls.

He seems absolutely elated about this situation, while I'm just trying to get my head to stop spinning. He can't be serious. I can't believe this is happening. What exactly does he expect me to do here? I'm not feeling so pissed off now, as I'm more intrigued.

Certainly, he doesn't expect me to fuck him and then fuck Ares too. I wonder if Ares is here to just observe or something. I'm sure watching and stuff has to be a normal happening around a biker club but how would I know

"Get on the bed," Ares barks, and I think I squeak.

I should probably speak up before who knows what happens. I give Ares a crazy look and then stare at 2 Piece, a little frightened. I know he'd never hurt me, but he should tell me what the hell's going on too.

I'm about two minutes from bolting. I won't be bossed around and used up like a club slut. Nothing against them or anything; it's just not how I roll.

Don't get me wrong, I'd love to get with Ares in a hot minute. However, I haven't been able to really be with anyone besides 2 Piece since we started this whole thing, whatever it is. I know we're just a random hookup when we see each other, but I've begun to develop feelings for him. I wasn't planning on it, but it just started to happen each time we'd meet up.

I find myself missing him more each time when we're apart. I know it's too soon and I know I'm stupid to develop feelings for a biker. We're completely different, I live one way and he lives another. I go to college full-time so I can get a degree to be an accountant. He rides his motorcycle, parties, and sleeps with random women, see nowhere near the same.

I gulp in air and draw on some courage. "I-I don't think I can do this. I'm sorry," I sputter, rushing back into the bathroom. I quickly close the door behind me, clicking the lock in place and slowly slide down to lean against the door.

Scrubbing my hands through my damp hair, I scream inside my head. Was he going to give me to Ares instead? How could he just call him in there and not talk to me about it? Clearly, I am not what he is used to.

Did he think he could just get me all turned on, give me an orgasm, then share me? How can he be so thoughtless? He obviously means more to me than I do to him. I know they pass club whores around, but I am not a fucking club whore.

I hear their voices through the door but can't make out what their saying. I shift so my ear's pressed against the door, hoping to catch some of what they are saying.

I can make out Ares better; his voice is deeper so it carries through the door. "I don't know, brother. You need to talk to her; she's a skittish thing. Appreciate you calling me in here though, wish she'd reconsider. We could have a lot of fun together" I hear some mumbling after that. "Good luck, brother." The bedroom door closes shortly after.

"Fuck." 2 Piece yells angrily and something slams against the wall.

"So fucking stupid." *Slam*. Goes something else.

"Had to fucking-fuck it up." *Slam*.

The door behind me rattles with the force of the bedroom door banging against the hinges as it's closed with force.

Exhaling, the tears start. I close my eyes tightly and rub at my cheeks. *I fucked it all up. He just said so. I didn't even have him yet and I already lost him.*

'Please Don't Judas Me' by Nazareth plays on his radio a few beats later; how freaking ironic. It just brings on the tears heavier with each word that I relate to.

2 Piece

I'm sitting at the bar, busily knocking back shots and attempting to drown out my fuck up. I'm a damn idiot for believing she'd be into it if Ares joined us. I thought she was comfortable enough with me to know I'd only do something to please her.

How could I have been so wrong? I've never messed up with a chick so badly. There haven't been many chicks at all in my life, but sex wise; I've never had an issue reading them.

When she shut the bathroom door I was a bit concerned but then she locked it as well. Hearing that tiny click felt magnified throughout the entire room and that's all I could hear, even seconds afterward. She felt conflicted enough she had to lock the door to keep me out. She'd never have to worry about me doing anything to hurt her. I may be a little rough around the edges, but when you hang around the brothers and club whores so much, it becomes a part of you.

I try to treat her with kid gloves, but when she gets snarky towards me, I forget that she's not used to this type of life. She's stubborn and can be a feisty bitch when she wants to be though. It's one of the things I enjoy most about her. I love it when a chick can handle her own, yet isn't afraid to ask her man for backup when needed.

I don't know how to deal with chicks emotions. I fuck, I don't date, and I don't marry. Damn it, I have to figure out a way to fix this somehow. She's a good girl and if I keep fucking it up, I really will end up alone forever. While I want to be free, at some point I want a bitch riding on the back of my bike with me.

Ares is a decent guy. He has his demons though, as we all do. From what little I've heard about him, he had a real shitty childhood.

The brothers said Ares' best friend found him locked in his basement when he was about fourteen years old. According to them, Ares was this tall gangly-looking kid who always got the shit beat out of him. He was dirty with raggedy clothes and covered in bruises and cuts.

He stayed with his friend until he was seventeen then somehow found the Oath Keepers MC. When Ares came to the club, he was full of anger and would go ballistic if he got into a fight. He became obsessed with working out and getting as big and strong as possible. The man's a goddamn giant beast now.

The brothers speak of the fights as if they were horror stories. Ares would try to rip body parts off the challenger while they were still alive. In the beginning, he'd break down after the fights. Now, he just zones out and becomes quiet.

He likes to zone out, so people never know what he's thinking or feeling. Ares' head is warped and Prez found it was best to have him as the Enforcer for the club. He's the perfect machine to get information or torture someone. Everyone wins—Ares gets to relieve his anger and the demons plaguing him inside, and the club gets their business handled.

He's become much better over the years and you can tell he uses sex as another type of outlet. He's dominant and enjoys having people watch, hell, I think it's a fucking turn on tool. I figured Avery might've agreed that it was hot as well, since she likes for me to get kinky with her.

Ares loves that stuff; he ties bitches up and spanks them and shit. He enjoys control and violence in club situations, but, at the same time, is often the voice of reason. I'm sure he's much more twisted when he's with certain women who enjoy it. Ares and I have also shared pussy quite a few times. He's not bisexual but we enjoy watching each other with a woman and having threesomes.

I hear a loud commotion and my gaze falls toward the main entry. What the fuck's going on now? Not enough alcohol on the planet for me at the moment, with all the damn drama.

"Prez!" Capone yells as soon as the door leading inside the club opens. He hobbles in, helping someone through the doorway. He seems fairly panicked and he's covered in blood. His arm is wrapped around Brently, and there is blood all over the front of Brently's shirt.

Fuck!

I hop off the barstool and move as quickly as possible to get to them. Reaching out, I help Brently. I'm a lot bigger than Capone is, so it will be easier for me.

"Fuck, Cap, go get the fucking Prez. He's going to freak the fuck out over this shit." Capone may be the weapons expert but my ass is closer to the head of the table than his is, so he has to follow my orders.

He nods and takes off down the hall towards the Prez's office. I help get Brently to a couch and lay him down.

"Fuck, man, what happened exactly?" I lift his shirt up high and carefully, trying not to touch what might be underneath.

Christ that has to hurt.

Spanning the width of his stomach and about six inches high, the word *SNAKES* has been tattooed. It could've been carved in for how angry the skin looks. It's bloody and surrounded in burn marks but there's no way that's the source of all this blood.

"What's all the blood from?" I grumble and frantically scan his body.

Brently takes a deep breath and winces. "It's not my stomach, there's a slice by my ribs under my arm pit. They said that they hope I'd bleed too much, that they know Dad and some Russian guy are sniffing around. Th-they wanted to pull my intestines out and braid them, crazy motherfuckers."

Double shit. This is so not good if the Twisted Snakes know we're checking into them. At least, I *guess* we're checking into them. I bet that's what those fucking looks were between Ares and Cain when I was asking to be filled in. Appears those assholes left out some shit when we had our chat.

I hear multiple footsteps come thundering down the hall, the sound echoing off the walls. I know it's Prez. He loves his kids so much; he's going to be heated about this shit.

I stand up to greet the storm I know is coming.

Prez's face is awash with worry and concern when he rounds the corner. "Brently? The fuck's going on here? 2, is that your blood? Where's my kid?" Prez scans the room as he barks a variety of questions. He can't see Brently since he's lying on the couch.

"Your kid's over on the couch. Fucking Snakes got to him." I nod toward the spot where Brently lays. Prez follows my motion, eventually seeing him.

"Motherfucker, give me a name, now." he snarls loudly and rushes to Brently's side.

I jump out of his way; he'll want to thoroughly check him over again. Capone comes to stand beside Prez, doing fuck all, not even twiddling his thumbs. It annoys the fuck out of me to see him basically standing around with his finger up his ass. Sometimes he acts like he doesn't know what the hell to do without a set of directions laid out.

"Capone, get a clean fucking bar towel, man," I growl and glower at him like he's a damn dimwit.

He nods and quickly snatches a towel off the long, polished oak bar top. We keep a folded pile right at the end of the bar. We're men; we spill shit all the time. Figured it was the most convenient place for them. I snatch it out of his hands and wad it up.

"Prez, put some pressure on that stab wound for him. I'll go get the med kit."

He peers over at me for a second and then down at my hands. He's lost in an angry haze clouding his mind. I wave the towel wad a few times before it clicks and gets through to him. I know he must be thinking a million things right now, processing what his next move should be. If it was my son, I'd be doing the same thing.

This is one of the main things you don't pull with the Oath Keepers MC. You don't fuck with members or their families. Ares and Twist are going to have a field day with these dumb fucks when we get ahold of them. No telling what their creative methods will be. Those Snakes have no clue just how twisted our Twist is; they haven't seen anything yet.

Prez snatches the wad from my grip and kneels next to Brently to apply some pressure on the gash. I'm going to need some ointment to put on those burns and the stitch kit. I hate doing this shit, but it's got to be done. It seems like I'm always the one patching people up.

"*Shit!*" Brently yelps when Prez lays the towel against his mutilated skin.

Poor dude, I bet that shit hurts like a bitch.

I make my way down the hall towards the bathroom. It's gray with four stalls and two sinks in it for when we have get-togethers and company. Nothing special, but it works. Digging through the closet, I grab my med kit med kit. It has the basics such as gauze, cotton balls, super glue, peroxide, alcohol swabs, Q-tips, needles, ointments, Ace bandages, thread, etc. for random injuries.

Snatching that up, I jog back to Brently.

He wheezes a few painful sounding breaths, panting through the pain. "*Fuck*, it hurts. How am I going to get rid of this ugly-ass tattoo?"

Capone and I both chuckle at that. Brently is a bigtime pretty boy. Now he has this ugly-ass tattoo and a gnarly gash that will end up leaving a sick looking jagged scar as well.

"Don't you worry 'bout that fuckin' tattoo, boy. I'm going to skin those little fuckers for this bullshit," Prez growls, his eyes shining with promises of payback.

"Dad, seriously, they're nasty guys. I don't want to see any of the members get hurt because of me."

Brently's a good kid, always keeping his nose clean. The guy should be away at college but instead he ended up deciding to stay local. Looking at Prez, it's hard to believe he even has a kid this old. I think he's in his late forties though.

"It's club business. You didn't want to be a part of it, so it's not your decision." Prez cuts him off and I nod, agreeing. He's been trying to get his son to be a part of the club for years now. "Capone, call Spin and tell him to get the fuck over here as soon as possible to look at this shitty tatt."

"Sure, Prez. I'm on it." Capone sits at the bar and pulls out his flip phone.

Good little minion. At least that will keep him busy for a while. Don't get me wrong, Capone's not a bad guy. He just comes off as naïve sometimes and it's annoying as fuck.

Hopefully Spin can get over here soon. I don't know what to do with that nasty looking tattoo besides clean it up; he should have a better idea.

Have to give this kid props, telling us to hold off on getting retribution. If it were me, I'd be pointing and shooting the first chance I got. Brently has some balls, laying here hurting and not seeking revenge.

Prez steps a few paces away and gets on the horn. I'm sure he's calling another fucking meeting. We can't seem to stay out of church here lately.

Dumping peroxide all over his stomach, it sizzles and Brently clenches his teeth, hissing. *Bet that burns like a bitch.* There's so much that needs fixing, and I'm no doctor. Thank God they didn't really gut him, or I wouldn't be able to help him at all.

"Ah shit!" He lets out a strangled yell after clenching his teeth for a few seconds.

I wince and mutter, "Sorry, bro. I have to get this shit cleaned up. There's no telling how dirty that shit was they used on you to do this." I pat it dry with the bloody towel and thread my needle. "Want anything for the sewing?"

"I already took something Capone gave me," he grumbles as he shakes his head.

Carefully, I begin sewing him up. "Well, deep breaths then and hold still. Don't want to fuck this up, or you'll have an even more jacked up scar." I sigh and attempt to concentrate on my task.

"It just hurts, bad, 2. Those guys were such dicks. I'm glad I wasn't at Mom's house or my sister's apartment. I couldn't imagine her or Princess getting hurt like this."

"I know, just try not to worry about it. Your dad will take care of things and make sure Mona and Princess are safe, he always has."

"That's one thing I do worry about though. I don't want my dad or any of you guys getting hurt, all because I fell for the wrong girl," he admits with a whisper, closing his eyes.

I can't blame the kid, falling for some good pussy. Speaking of, I wonder if Avery's feeling better now. I need to check on her and fix my fuck-up.

I'd hate to have to go through what Brently does with his woman. Being kept away from the chick I want would drive me mad. It's bad enough Avery lives far away; in Tennessee and that I have to put up a front so people will leave me the fuck alone about it. I mean, I don't have to front, but I do anyhow.

"It's all good, kid; a lot of us have fucked up somehow when it comes to females." I finish the last stitch, wipe around the sewed-up area and wrap his wound in some sterile gauze. "All set. Just make sure you keep it clean. If it starts oozing or anything fucked up like that, go to the doc. Yeah?" He nods.

I grab his hand and help pull him to sit up carefully.

"Ah." He groans, scrunching up his face in pain while laying his hand over the gash I just sewed up.

"Go easy on touching that shit. You don't want to fuck-up the stitches. Trust me, the second round of stitches are no joke," I scold.

Ares and Cain come rushing into the room.

"The fuck's up, boss?" Ares' gaze goes straight to Prez "I called Twist and Smiles. They're on their way in here now."

"Good. Capone is at the bar and Spin is on his way too. That's enough for an emergency vote. The other brothers running behind will have to be caught up later. Cain, go call Niko to come to the club so I can fill in everyone at once. Ares, call the Nomads when we're out of church and tell them it may be time to ride in."

Cain walks to the side and quickly pulls his phone out.

"Sure, boss. No problem. You want them all here?" Ares asks as Twist and Smiles come walking in.

"Ah, no, just call Nightmare and Exterminator for now. Those big boys should be the right kind of force I need for this issue." Prez heads to the bar and grabs a bottle of Johnny Walker Red and a tumbler. "Everybody get the fuck to church." he booms and Twist jumps.

He gets crazy eyes for a minute then takes off for church. Twist doesn't like yelling; it seems to trigger something in him and sometimes he flips out. Today wouldn't be a good day for him to lose it.

I shift closer to Prez and lean in so nobody knows my business. "Prez. I need to check on something really quick."

"2, it's time for church, brother." He gives me a once-over and turns back toward Brently.

"Yeah, I get it, but I need to peek my head in my room," I argue stubbornly.

87

"The fuck you do. That shit can wait. This is muthafuckin' club business and it's time for church. Other bullshit gets dealt with after church."

I know he's pissed because his son's hurt so I nod and head in with the other guys. It irritates the fuck out of me, but Prez deserves my respect and compliance so I shake it off. I know if it were me, I'd want immediate action.

I'll have to do some major ass kissing to Avery at this point. I should've stayed in my room until she came out. Jesus, did I dig myself into a mess with her or what? I'm not cut out for this woman shit. You'd think I learned something from my sister, but nope. She didn't date much growing up, because I'd chase the losers off.

Fucking women. Shaking my head, I take my place at the table. I chin-lift to my brothers and give the head of the table my full attention. It's time for club business and that is something that I understand.

Avery

Sitting up off the floor, I scrub my hands down my face. *Fuck, I must've passed out after my crying fit.* I haven't been doing anything really, but that car ride from Tennessee must've worn me out. Sixteen hours in a truck with only pee breaks is a bit overwhelming. I feel like I've ran a marathon, especially with my tidal wave of emotions.

2 Piece is most likely asleep in his room. I bet he thinks I'm a hot-ass mess, locking him out of his own bathroom. I smack my lips a few times.

Ugh, I need something to drink.

My face feels swollen and my hair like it's shooting off in every direction. I stand up and lean over the sink to stare into the mirror. Yep. I look like a freaking monster. I have Medusa hair and dried slobber on part of my left cheek.

Twisting on the cold water, I let my hands sit under it for a moment to help wake me up. Cupping my hands, I wash my face and attempt to pat down my hyperactive hair.

Deep breaths. I silently chant a few times to myself.

Okay, time to pull myself together and go out there. I want to see how he acts or if he's asleep. Hopefully, we can talk this over and everything will be good again. I don't want him to disappear from my life when he's barely in it as it is.

Opening the bathroom door, I check around the room, glancing at the bed first—nope, empty—and the corner chair—empty too. *Shit.* He never came back to the freaking room.

I bet that fucking asshole went and found another girl! To think I was feeling bad and sorry for flipping out so much. He has some damn nerve, I swear. I came all this way from Tennessee, for him to do this shit to me?

Oh hell no, I don't fucking think so.

Leaving the room, I storm through the clubhouse. I'll give him a piece of my mind once and for all. He'll learn not to make a damn fool out of me. He doesn't like drama? Well, he hasn't even seen drama yet!

Turns out, he's nowhere to be found. He's not in the kitchen, the bar, the bathroom, nowhere. Men can be so infuriating. Of course out of all of them, I have to pick a bullheaded biker.

The only person I saw out in the bar was some young guy on the couch with a bandage wrapped around his chest. He was good-looking too. He seemed a few years younger than me though.

Poor guy looked miserable. I bet whatever happened to him hurt pretty badly. He probably wrecked his motorcycle or something. There was also an awful looking tattoo on him too. *Yuck.*

Fuck this shit, I'm calling Nikoli and telling him all about this crap. If anything, 2 will get his ass beat for being a dick and leaving me like he did. I might like cocks, but I damn sure won't date one.

I step out the main door and into the Texas warmth. God, even at nighttime this place stays warm. So far, I love it here.

I can see why London was so happy to come back. She's lucky to have Cain in her life. I wonder if I'll ever have what she has. Well, not exactly the same, but just someone to grow old with at least. I don't want the fifty kids they'll probably end up having. Maybe one, someday down the road, but that's it.

I pull my Galaxy S7 out and find Niko's picture, then press the call icon forcefully. Yep, pressing it hard makes me feel a little better. It rings twice then he picks up. It sounds like he's driving, there's a little echo and noises like he's rolling up the window.

"Yes, Bean?"

"Niko, I need you to come get me from the club, please."

"Okay, I am coming now."

"Thank you so much. See you soon."

"Yes," he absently responds and hangs up.

Niko's the type who'll text you all day long, but he hates talking on the phone with a passion. I guess probably because he's a man and they all say they don't care for it. I think Niko likes to be able to read your expression and the way things are said, so he can react appropriately.

I'm glad I don't come from another country and have to worry about speaking another language, or learning to read people's different body language and stuff. It must be such a pain in the ass for him. I've never thought of that before. I'll have to stop giving him so much crap about it.

Anyhow, back to that asshole. I'm going to tell Nikoli everything. He's my best friend and I have no problems sharing with him.

Gravel crunches and I glance up, seeing truck approach. He speeds through the lot as soon as the prospect opens the gate. The shape of the truck's headlights gives him away instantly. The Silverado's are nice trucks, his drove like a Cadillac the entire trip here.

He parks quickly and jumps out, appearing flustered and rushed. I wonder what he was up to. Maybe he met a girl? Could everyone be finding booty calls in Texas? Well, everyone but me obviously.

"Yes, Bean, what is happening?" He seems way too upset for just a little call from me. I mean, he got that I was that upset from just a few words? He's crazy good. No wonder he and Tate can communicate with just certain looks.

"I have to tell you what happened with 2 Piece," I sigh dramatically and go into detail about everything that had gone down. "I can't believe you got that I was so upset from just a few words on the phone. You're good, you." I wink and he shakes his head, his gaze stern.

"No. Cain called first. I was on my way, and then you call too."

"Oh."

"Yeah, shit fucked up," he mutters earnestly and it peaks my interest.

"What's going on?" I try to come off nonchalantly with a breezy attitude. Hopefully, he won't think I'm being too nosey and he'll tell me. I know he had business here, but I have no clue what it is.

"I do not know. First, I teach 2 Piece manners, and then I speak to their leader." He treks past me to the door and I practically run to keep up with his powerful legs.

I'm clapping inside because I can't wait to see Niko punch 2 Piece. Fucker wants to hurt me; I'll get my best friend to teach him not to be so rude to me. 2 and I could've worked everything out just fine without Ares, but he chose to take off and get with who knows who. This club will get a nice little taste of drama, and it'll take a while for him to forget about me.

"Where is Cain?" Niko asks the cute guy on the couch.

If it wasn't for the nasty gash-like marks on his tummy, his stomach would be phenomenal. He could've been a model before he mutilated himself. He doesn't look like he's a biker. I wonder if maybe he did that stuff to himself to get into the club.

I bet you have to do some crazy shit to join. The brothers I saw earlier in the garage were all good-looking, but also had a sinister kink to them.

The guy appears surprised when Niko speaks to him. "Oh, um, they'll be out in just a minute. Are you Niko?"

"Yes," he scoffs.

Geez, you can tell Niko's pissed; he's normally very friendly when he meets someone for the first time. My fluffy man-kitten is strutting around with his chest out like a blond bear about to pounce. I want to feel sorry for 2 Piece, but I'm not quite there yet.

Right as the guy answers Niko, the door opens and out walk a group of huge bikers. Fuck, do they eat steroids in their oatmeal every morning here? I feel like they should be on a beach commercial for board shorts instead of leather.

They look mean, but they're hot as fuck. I wonder if I turned on some Beach Boys' songs, if these bikers would strip down to their underwear and play some backyard football. I could use a good show.

As soon as 2 Piece comes through the door, Niko's on him. Niko snatch's his shirt by the neck and slams 2 into the wall behind him. He stretches the shirt material out as 2 Piece's chest and shoulder muscles contract, ready to defend himself. Niko's biceps bulge as he prepares to rain destruction with his fists.

"Hey, man, what the fuck?" 2 Piece shouts in surprise. His arms shoot up in a placating gesture.

Niko growls down at him. "You upset Bean; I hurt you," he snarls ferociously and lets loose a solid body shot right into 2 Piece's stomach.

"Son of a bitch!" 2 roars and it appears as if they may kill each other.

Ares and Prez quickly move into action and attempt to separate them.

*Ah...*witnessing 2 Piece getting hit hurts me inside. I didn't think it would affect me this way. Fuck, I hope he's okay. I can't believe I was such a fool to let Niko hurt him.

Who am I kidding? I don't let him do anything. He's powerful enough to do anything he wants to. I try to move closer to Nikoli.

"N-no, Niko, please, just stop. I'm sorry I got you so upset, but don't hurt him anymore." I plead with Niko but manage to stay out of their way.

They're men and I'm not stupid enough to jump into the middle of something like this. I could get hit and that would hurt immensely with these big, burly men. They both feel as if they have something to prove to each other at this point. Niko will want to show that he'll defend his friends and 2 Piece, that he won't be disrespected in his club in front of his brothers.

God, what have I done? I may have just gotten one of them killed. I'm such a damn fool.

Niko begins to calm down and takes a step back after getting a decent hit in. His head held high, proud Russian cheekbones flushed, he stood up for me and is strutting as if he's an ancient warrior.

The brothers relax; dropping their arms and take a step back from blocking the two angry men.

"I don't fucking think so, Russian." 2 declares, pissed off and rushes toward Nikoli. He tackles Niko around the waist and they go flying to the floor in a heap of flailing arms and legs, attempting to get in the better position.

I can't see. Fuck, I don't know what's going on. Ugh, there are too many bikers around them.

I raise my voice amongst the chaos, hoping to be heard and helped. "Move, somebody stop them, damn it. They're going to kill each other, please. Niko! 2 Piece!" I shove against some tall biker to try to get him out of my way. He spins around and glares down at me.

I glance up and am met with one steel-grey iris and one sapphire blue iris. He looks straight up evil. He snarls and I duck beside a different biker.

These fuckers are going to let Niko and 2 kill each other. I see Cain and head over to him as fast as I can. "Please, Cain, please get them. Niko will hurt him," I declare desperately, and pull on Cain's massive arm.

He smirks down at me. "Look, Avery, I step in and attempt to separate them in a bit, but you have to let them tire each other out for a few minutes, babe. I'm not about to get hit or some dumb shit." He shoulders me off and faces back toward the fight, effectively blocking my view again.

Fucking bikers!

"Ah!" I let loose a high-pitched scream and I swear it's like a freeze button. Everyone turns toward me and halts, staring at me with wide eyes. 2 Piece and Niko are wrapped around each other on the floor peering over at me like I just got stabbed or something.

"Please," I whimper.

Niko stands up, adjusts his clothes and holds his hand out to 2 to help him up. 2 Piece looks at it for a second, glancing at Nikoli's face, then takes it and stands up. His nose is bleeding badly; it's swollen with a greenish purple hue and Niko has a cut above his eyebrow. He looks handsome but flushed. I'm sure their faces are going to be black and blue tomorrow.

Great, just fucking awesome.

I had no idea I'd be so conflicted inside about either of them getting hurt. I never guessed my stomach would be in knots and I would want to puke. I figured Niko would punch 2 Piece one good time and yell at him, then that would be the end of it.

I didn't think they'd roll around on the ground like wild savages attempting to kill each other, while everyone stood around watching like it's cable TV. *Fucking dicks.*

"Y'all are a bunch of fucking dicks, for letting them beat the shit out of each other," I spit angrily witnessing the two people I care so deeply for, injured and no one stopped it.

My muscles begin to tingle and feel like Jell-O, my adrenaline starting to crash. I wrap my arms in front of me, trying to ward off the sudden chill I feel spread through my body. My eyes begin to fill with tears.

Fuck. Fuck. Fuck. Jerk-offs got me ready to cry. Just great, I swear. I turn toward the hall and rush to the bathroom. I refuse to cry or puke in front of a room full of men.

Shutting the door quickly, I check through the room as I make my way to the sink. Not bad, it's all grey and boring but clean. Everything in this clubhouse is grey it seems: the concrete floors, the walls, the metal separators between the toilets, and the outside of the building—all of it. If it wasn't for the bar being oak and the couches being black leather, I'd suspect they're all color-blind.

Grasping the counter tightly, I stare into the mirror. I can't believe I'm spending the day locked in bathrooms. Thank God I didn't attempt to wear makeup today. That would've been a massive disaster with all of my bawling I seem to be doing.

Taking in my tearstained face once again, I shake my head in disgust at myself. *Well, you found him after all Avery, and fucked it up all over again.* I cup my hands and wash my face once more, as I let the hot tears stream down my cheeks and chin, coating my skin in saltiness.

2 Piece

"What the fuck is your problem, motherfucker?" I glower toward Niko, panting.

This idiot just jumped me for no fucking reason, and I'm about five seconds from putting a bullet in him if he doesn't have a legit reason for it.

"Me? You must be kidding, biker. You treat Avery like whore, then question me for defending her. I will crush you, you little Oath fuck," he barks and I have to stop myself before I cause a rift between us and the Russians, due to me killing him.

"Treat her like a whore?" I reply incredulously. "I've never treated her like some fucking whore, you Russian twat. It was a goddamn misunderstanding and she freaked the fuck out before we could talk about it like rational adults. I didn't know you were her personal guard dog. Does she fuck you to pay you too?" I snap back, glaring in anger.

I thought these two were over with a long time ago, before we first hooked up. Now this fool's here acting like she's his girl and shit. Do they still fuck? She told me it was only me now. She better not be lying, I don't fuck with liars or druggies. Dealt with that shit too much growing up; I won't go back there again.

"Pay me with fuck? No, you horse ass, she is hung up on biker dick from what I hear. Now who is going to tell me why I was called?" He turns his shoulder from me and gazes at the brothers.

I swear to Christ, if he responds sarcastically one more time I'm going to throat punch this motherfucker. I may be smaller than his ass by about two inches, but that makes me the perfect height to hit him low. I'm not some bitch; around here you earn your respect. The brothers are friendly and shit, but you have to prove yourself that you won't take shit from nobody.

"You telling me that she called you, upset about some shit and you drove over here to threaten me? All because she's hung up on me? She knows this is just a good time, it's always been that way."

This woman is going to be the damn death of me, just watch. I knew she wouldn't be able to separate this after so long. She's a woman, and women tend to get attached more quickly than men. I'm not going to lie; I have some feelings for her too.

I didn't realize we were going to start to move in this direction though. I mean, Christ, she lives in a whole other state. Figures I'd pick a bitch to start having feelings for and she'd live sixteen hours away.

I'm going to have to talk to her about this. I need to find out what her true feelings are for me and if I want to give it a go with her. It's been a long time since I had a chick to call my own. After earlier though, I don't know if she can even handle this lifestyle.

"Yes. That is what I said. Any good vodka here?" he asks, friendly now, and just like that, Niko has moved past this fiasco.

I on the other hand...it's just starting to sink in. It's hitting me like a kick to the nuts. I mean, Avery's a good girl. She's fun, smart, gorgeous, and I like being around her. She's been right in front of me this whole time and I never even noticed what could be.

I'll have to show her I can be what she wants. But what does she even want? I know fucking next to nothing about what she desires or cares about. I'm a damn idiot. I've got to get my head out of my ass or she's going to pass me right on by.

I gesture to the bar. "Yeah, man, there's vodka." I nod at the prospect, and he rushes over to the bar to get Niko his tumbler of Absolute on the rocks.

"Hey, Scratch, get me a beer too," Ares pipes up, and I fix my clothes.

I always forget this dude's name. Hell, I was called prospect the entire time until I got patched, so it won't hurt 'em.

Pull yourself together and find her.

"Thank you, biker." Niko sits at the bar and takes a sip.

The prospect nods, face full of shaggy hair, and hands Ares his bottle of Budweiser as well.

"I'm going to go check on Avery, make sure she's straight," I grumble and pat down my shirt. I can feel it's stiff with blood in certain spots. At least it's a black shirt..

"She was sad. I do not like her sad; fix it, 2 Piece."

I roll my eyes at Nikoli and he smirks. This Russian is going to be a pain in my ass.

Heading toward the hallway, I go searching her out. I don't even know what to say to make it any better. I probably shouldn't start with something like, 'Hey, sorry you got your friend on me to kick my ass.'

I feel bad, and I know I can be a dickhead, but I don't roll over either.

Once I come to the locked bathroom door, I place my ear against it and I can hear her sniffles through the thin wood. The muscles in my stomach clench, knowing that I need to do some major ass kissing. I can't believe Shorty's in there crying over me right now. I must actually mean something to her.

How did this shit spin out of control? It went from us having fun, to both of us storming away, to getting into a fight and making her cry. I can't stand drama, and this is turning right straight into drama fucking city.

"Shorty, come on; open the door, babe." I rest by forearms on the doorframe and speak against the wood so she can hear me and I don't have to yell.

She sniffles then she blows her nose.

"No," she utters softly, stubbornly.

There's my feisty girl. She's upset but still her normal stubborn ass. Good, make me beg, babe. I deserve it right now.

"Come on, free bird, open up," I pry a little louder this time.

"No, and stop calling me pet names," she hiccups and I chuckle to myself. She's fucking adorable, giving me stomach flutters and shit, not just in my nuts.

"Open this fuckin' door, Avery Marie, or I'll bust it the fuck down. You don't want me breaking any doors right now either, baby. I'm already all spun the fuck out from that bullshit your boy put me through in there in front of my brothers. Pissing me off any more is *not* the right way to go about this. I came over here to check on you and apologize; don't start up no more shit," It leaves me in a growl.

Just as I'm about to start pounding on the door, I hear a small click and the door cracks open. I peek through the small sliver and see her face is red, blotchy, and tearstained, her nose swollen as well.

"Okay, geesh," she murmurs, backing away from the door.

I push through and lock the door again behind me. My heart hurts for her right now. I hate seeing her upset like this.

"Shorty." I cringe and pull her to my chest. I'm such a fucking piece of shit to make her cry like this.

She sniffles and wipes her nose with her hand. She's so damn sweet, and I can't help but look at her differently after my revelation earlier. I'm an asshole and need to make this better with her.

"It's okay; I'm fine," she mumbles and clears her throat, but she isn't close to being fine. She's all down and out.

"Shit, Shorty, I'm not dumb enough to not know what fine actually means when it comes to a woman. You're upset, and I'm a dick. You made your point clear, now talk to me so we can fix this."

She leans back a little and gazes up at me with those wide, honey eyes that warm me inside. "Umm, you mean w-we can fix this? I thought you'd be hating me right about now and kicking me out of the club."

"Nah, Shorty. I couldn't hate you 'cause you freaked and weren't comfortable. I didn't grasp that we weren't on that level or I never would've called Ares in to have some fun with us."

"What do you mean with us?" She cocks her head and raises an eyebrow.

"You know, join in. I thought it would bring you more pleasure, having the two of us. I'd never ask him, if I didn't already trust him and know he would respect you."

"Wait, you did that for me? You weren't trying to pass me around to your brothers?" Her eyes widen in surprise and I scrunch up my face.

Fuck, I can't believe I didn't think of that. Of course, she would get that impression. She doesn't know how everything works in the club.

"What the actual fuck? Hell, no, baby. My brothers don't touch shit unless we agree or say it's cool. Ares and I are good when it comes to that sort of thing, so I don't mind him. I wouldn't invite any other brothers in with us."

"You wanted to have a threesome with me and Ares? Shit, I'm an idiot," she shakes her head, rubbing her temples

"Yeah, Avery, I would never pass you off like that. You're not some club whore and I would never treat you as one. I have way too much respect for ya', babe."

She beams a bright smile at me and I return it with one of my own. She's so damn gorgeous, just that smile alone turns me on.

"I'm sorry I flipped out and locked myself in your bathroom. I know you would never hurt me. I was just really confused and hurt."

"It's all good, Shorty, I'm sorry for not sticking around and making sure you were straight earlier." I tuck her in tight against my chest. I love how she feels against me, in my arms. Inhaling deeply, I smell her sweet, girly-smelling hair. "Damn, baby, you bring your own shampoo this time?"

"Yeah, I always steal yours when I visit, so I brought mine this time." She grins cheekily.

"I like my smell on you though," I grumble as I take her mouth with mine. She tips her face up eagerly and returns my kiss.

Her lips are needy and it spurs me on more. Palming her left breast, I tweak her nipple. She has me all turned up and ready for her with only one kiss.

"Mm…2, I want you. Just you right now, maybe Ares can join us another time? As long as it's together and not me with him, alone," she whispers breathlessly, and I want to eat her up. She's absolutely intoxicating.

"Yeah, Avery, you got me, Shorty." My hands skim over her curves, until I reach the button on her shorts.

I unclasp them and shove the material down with eagerness. Kissing her once, quick and hard, I pull back and spin her around. Then I push her toward the counter and sinks, putting pressure on her back until she bends over.

"Hold onto the counter tightly, Avery. This is going to be rough and fast. I'll take you again later to make up for it, I promise." I rumble and undo my jeans button with one hand, eager to feel her around me.

Pulling my cock free, I pump it twice, grasping and flexing my hand at the tip. Gripping my wallet with my other hand, I stick the leather in my mouth to assist in digging a condom out.

"Shorty, turn back around a minute and slide this on my dick." She complies, spinning toward me and taking the condom.

She drops to her knees and I grit my teeth, picturing her taking my cock deep in her mouth. She lines the condom up with the tip and pushes it on about an inch. She leans forward and rolls the condom using her tongue and lips while taking my cock into her mouth as if she could read my mind.

Tingles spread rapidly all over my body making me shudder. My groin tightens and I can feel myself dripping pre-cum into the condom, Avery has me so ready. She makes little slurp sounds and I'm about to explode..

"Fuck, babe." Yanking her up quickly under her arms, I turn her to face the counter. "Over, now!" I gasp, pushing her to brace herself.

She grins, bending down and holds onto each side of the counter. I want inside her so bad, I'm shaking like a crack addict. Grabbing my cock roughly, I squeeze it in anticipation.

Yes.

Spreading her ass cheeks so I can see the pretty little ass and her pussy, I rub the tip of my cock on her core, coating it in her juices. She squirms and lets out a little mewling sound. My abs contract, flexing tightly as I slide inside and grip firmly onto her hips.

"You think you can control this?" she puffs.

"Baby, I know I control this."

"Ah, Jesus."

Yep. I'm fuckin' God and you're going to remember this for the rest of your life. I reach forward and wrap one hand around her delicate neck, then give it a gentle squeeze and I feel her swallow.

"Please, 2." Avery begs, and I love every minute of it.

I hold onto her hip with my other hand and scoot in close to her so my body heat washes over her and warms her back. Rocking my hips back, I slam into her the same time as I flex my fingers around her throat.

"God, yes," she screams, her voice muddled by my hand and I replicate my movements a few more times.

"I feel your perfect pussy squeezing me, Shorty, you gonna' come like my good girl?" I squeeze her hip again with my other hand and she grinds back into me.

This pussy's so damn hungry and I plan to give it exactly what it so badly wants. "I got you, babe," I grit, panting and start hammering into her. She lets out little whimpers with every thrust.

Running my hand from her hip to her breast, I squeeze and play with her stiff peaks. Her pussy starts to spasm, gripping my cock frantically. She moans and I tighten my palm, effectively silencing her into a soundless moan. Pulling nearly all the way out to my tip, then I slam home three times, feeling myself go off like a damn volcanic eruption.

"Fuck me, that's so good," Groaning, I dump every drop I have into her core.

Avery

And that is one of the reasons why 2's so special to me—above any other old Joe-shmo. He knows exactly what I love when it comes to sex. No other guy has quite gotten it, but 2 Piece hits it right every time.

I've never been so sexually compatible with a man before. It'll happen like that over and over with him, until I can't feel my legs anymore. He's by far the most erotic, dangerous, most talented man in bed, I've ever been with.

He has other things that stand out to me, other than the sex. His confidence, for example, he seems so sure of himself and knows he has it going on. It's refreshing; the guys I go to school with are all patsies or tools.

Maybe it's because most guys I go to class with are all math nerds. They're too spineless and dorky to compete. There's nothing wrong with that; just not my type.

Then there's the hot guys I've dated from school...they're all douche canoes or moochers. When you see 2 Piece, he screams 'I don't give a fuck what you think.' I envy that. I wish I didn't care so much what my mom thinks and about the shit she's always put me through.

I wash my hands thoroughly again in the sink. I hate the smell of condoms. For some reason, they have a strange odor to me and leave a weird feeling on my fingers.

2 Piece does the same, smirking at me while washing his. His cock's still semi-hard, taunting me. He's an arrogant ass, I swear. Why do I find that so damn cute?

"Where'd you go when you left the room, anyhow?" I peer over at him, curiously.

I can't help but wonder if he was with the other guys or if there were females around as well. I don't understand why I'm territorial over him. I hate having jealous feelings. But, the thoughts of him being with another woman eat away in the back of my mind. It makes me want to climb the walls.

"I was in church," he shrugs.

"That's the room you came out of? You were praying with all those other guys?"

He chuckles and smiles at me like I'm amusing. "Nah, Shorty. Church is like a 'meeting' to discuss club shit. Not sure praying would do some of us any good."

"Oh wow, I had no idea," my cheeks heat.

I hate being so naïve about his club, but I can't help it. It's fascinating and I want to learn everything about it that I can. "What do you guys talk about in there?"

"I can't discuss club shit with you. I'm sure London's told you we don't share club business with anyone," he mutters, becoming a touch defensive.

"No, I never asked her before, and she's never said anything. I won't tell anyone if that's the issue."

"No, I believe you wouldn't say anything, but I just can't. I'll tell you one thing though, so you can stay smart and safe. The kid on the couch is the President's son, and someone screwed with him. That's why Niko's here and that's why you need to be careful if you leave the club or London's house. You hear?"

"Okay, I'll be careful. I already promised Niko I'd behave and stay out of the way, but if you need any help, just ask."

"All right, Avery enough about this. Let's get out to the bar, I want a drink. I'm sure you must be hungry by now too."

As soon as he mentions food my stomach grumbles. I haven't eaten since way earlier. It must have not been bothering me because I've been either excited or upset.

"I'm starving and not-like -eat-half-a-cow-but-a-whole-one starving," I share with a grin. He wraps his arm around me and walks me out of the bathroom then down the hallway.

"You, can eat a whole cow, huh? There're some bags of chips behind the bar you can have, but no cow. We do need to try and keep you energized though."

Keep me energized, hmm? It sounds like it's going to be a fun night. We get to the bar and nearly everyone has cleared out. I notice the guy on the couch 2 Piece was talking about and also the scary guy from earlier.

Snuggling closer to 2, I wrap my hands around him, so I'm hugging him to me and I can bury my face in his chest.

"Hey, Shorty, what's up?" he mutters and gently lifts my chin with his finger.

Since when did I become this shy, quiet chick? I'm always loud and bouncing around. It's pretty intimidating being inside a clubhouse with a bunch of beefy bikers everywhere.

"Um, nothing. It's just that, well, the guy speaking to the President's son is kind of scary. He wasn't exactly friendly when you were fighting with Niko. He'd glared at me like he was going to step on me or something. Oh shit, is Nikoli okay? Where is he?"

"I don't know, he's probably doing something about a problem we're dealing with right now. And yes he's fine, still an asshole Russian though."

I shove against his stomach when he talks about Niko and then find a spot at the bar. I scooch onto one of the stools and. 2 Piece pushes my legs apart gently, coming to stand between them. He cages me in with his hands resting on the counter behind me.

When he bites his bottom lip; all I can imagine is him eating my pussy, while I stare at his sexy mouth. He leans in and kisses the tip of my nose and I blink. That was so saccharine; no one ever kisses me sweetly like that.

I lick my lips and give him a small smile in return; he's pretty damn perfect in my eyes. However, h needs to back off from Niko. I can't have the guy I care for and my best friend fighting with each other, that won't fly with me.

"Nikoli's my best friend. You need to be nice," I declare and give him *the look*.

"It's all good, free bird. And Spin? What the fuck? Spin's easy going, baby."

"Uh, no. Pretty sure he's a jerk, if the look he gave me was any indication."

He huffs and turns toward the hot, mean guy, "Spin, the fuck you do to my girl over here?"

Spin turns and flashes a yummy smile, looking guilty like he got caught with his hand in the cookie jar.

Oh, he has dimples! I love dimples.

"I didn't do a fucking thing, bro. Bitch was trying to jump in the mix and get people hit and shit." He sounds just like Jax from *Sons of Anarchy* and I swear my panties are going to melt right the fuck off. He looks nothing like him, but sweet Lord, that voice.

"Ah, gotcha'," 2 Piece nods and faces me, looking like he just solved world hunger.

"What exactly was that, just now?" I scrunch up my nose.

"What?" He grabs a beer and a bag of Doritos, then sits at the bar next to me.

"Uh, that whole three-word conversation y'all just had. What was that? I don't see how that resolved anything at all. It was just weird."

"Nah, Shorty, you were trying to jump into shit. You're lucky he didn't lock your ass in a closet somewhere."

A closet, no, I don't think so. I totally would've bitten his fine ass if he tried that shit.

"Yeah right, locked me in a closet- ha." I roll my eyes and chuckle to myself.

"Avery, I'm serious. You try to get into the middle of some shit and a brother will lock you up to keep you safe. Baby, you're so little. Could you imagine if Niko or I hadn't seen you and hit you by accident? We don't hit to play around; we do it to cause some damage. I'd never forgive myself if you got hurt like that, because of me."

Well, I understand the logic, but it doesn't mean I have to like it. I nod. I'm not trying to have an entire new fight tonight.

"Come on, free bird, grab your chips and let's go to the room. I'll keep Ares out, I promise."

Cheeky fucker.

"Gee thanks. But, I wouldn't mind him coming around now, if you're in the mix." I wink.

He flashes a wolfish grin. "Cool, Shorty, if you're really down, then I'll tell him what's up. You'll enjoy yourself, I promise."

I smirk and nod again.

If I'm down, are you kidding me? Having two gorgeous men taking me, at the same time? Not much of a decision to make there.

His smile grows at my exaggerated nodding. "I don't think you know what you're getting yourself into, baby."

"I guess you'll just have to show me, huh, big boy?"

He chuckles loudly and pulls me along into his room.

2 Piece

One week later...

"Avery Marie, just pick out the damn candy bar you want and let's fucking roll out already. You've been staring at that candy display for a good three minutes."

She sends me an irritated look, as if I'm the one in the wrong. Yet it's her ass that's been being stubborn and not picking a damn candy out. I understand there're fifty different ones to choose from, but come on.

I personally prefer Three Musketeers. Grabbing one for myself, it'll be the perfect snack for tonight after I have my fun with her. She usually enjoys ice cream after we've fucked. I like chocolate or a sandwich.

She's usually too tired afterward to make me a sandwich though, so I've developed a bad candy habit. I've started hitting the gym room with Cain the past few days to help with that problem. I can't have my baby pinch me in any other spots, teasing about more of me to hold on to. *Crazy damn woman.*

I'm sick of waiting, so I huff, "Fine, Shorty, I'll pick five of those bitches and you can have the one you want out of those."

If anything, I'll eat what she doesn't. I go to reach for a few candy bars and she snatches my wrist.

Peering over, I shoot her a 'what the fuck look'. Has this bitch lost her fuckin' mind?

She whispers and I lean a little closer so I can hear her. "Shh, I'm taking forever because that creepy dude over there's been staring and following us around the store."

I start to glance up to find the dude she's worried about, but she squeezes my hand tighter. "No, don't look now. He'll know I said something."

"I don't give a flying fuck what any cocksucker thinks. I'll squash a dipshit with my boot if he starts tripping," I hiss and glance wherever the fuck I want to.

Fuck, no way. She wasn't kidding.

There's no mistaking the guy whose busy staring at us. He's wearing a cut that has a large patch with green snakes twisted together. *Motherfucker. Shit.*

Relinquish

Glancing towards the opposite side, I see *Joker* stitched on his name patch. He looks like a fucking joker all right. Pale white skin, shaved head with short blond hair and pale eyes.

He cocks his head in return as I look him over, and glowers. *I don't fucking think so.* I lift my top lip and snarl back.

"We need to go, baby. I don't know if asshat over there has any buddies with him. Put your candy down and come on." I grab her arm and stare him down while we walk out. "Call Niko and tell him to call Prez and let them know we have a reptile problem in town."

"Okay," she mumbles, panicked, as she glances around and quickly shuffles out of the grocery store. She pulls her phone out of her back pocket and calls straight away as we walk to my black hog.

I climb on and she jumps on behind me with my assistance. She's gotten better at riding, but she's still not great. I take one of my pieces out of the back holster and slip it down into my boot. You never know if this fucker is feeling froggy or not.

"Give it to me to hold. I don't want it to fall out of your boot." She orders.

I must say that surprises the fuck out of me. I can't believe the thought of my gun doesn't make Avery squeamish in the least bit. I pull it back out in plain sight, so the Snake can see I'm not screwing around.

I hand it over to Avery and then lay on the throttle. I have a feeling I'm going to have to cruise around for a long time if I don't want him to follow me back to the club.

"Hold on tight, Shorty. If he gets too close, I'm going to have to lose him."

She scoots in closer and her arms tighten into an iron grip. She has more muscle in those skinny arms than I'd expected. I know she's scared, she's quiet and Avery's a fucking chatterbox around me when it's just the two of us. She likes to talk over my shoulder when we ride and I just listen.

I feel her face scrunched into my back like she's hiding, I don't blame her either. She knows something crazy is going on at the club, especially if we're calling the Russians to come and help out. Prez wants immediate retaliation. Luckily, Ares could talk him down a little.

Once the Nomads get into town, though, there's no holding back. The Nomads should be rolling in today or tomorrow and they mean business. With the names Exterminator and Nightmare, I'd be scared to be on the receiving end of a confrontation with any of those guys.

"He's still behind us," Avery yells out and tucks her head into my back again.

"Babe, stop looking back there. I have mirrors that can see him." I holler back and concentrate on the road in front of us.

I wonder what his plan is, following me around. I give the throttle some more juice and pick up speed. The wind

119

chops through my hair, and I feel Avery's fingers flex against my abs. The bike vibrates through my body as I grip the handles tightly and the rumble of the engine grows with the extra shot of fuel sent to it.

I glance to the mirror. That fucker is getting closer; I knew this wasn't some friendly visit. A high-pitched scream rings out from Avery and I have to stop myself from swerving.

"Ah, shit, he has a gun, 2 Piece. Go, go, go!"

As soon as her words register, I give it even more gas and roar down the busy street. My gut compresses in anticipation of what's to come. A spike of adrenaline kicks in and I weave in and out of traffic, trying to calm my shaking and not throw Avery off the back.

The blaring sounds of horns go off all around us. The drivers probably think I'm some thuggish biker driving around like an irresponsible fuckwit. If these people only knew that I was trying to get away from a gun, they'd most likely shit themselves.

I'd throw my finger to the idiot honking at us if my mind wasn't elsewhere. You don't honk at people in Texas, especially a goddamn biker. Your ass could end up shot or in a fist fight.

I'm too busy attempting to dodge this Snake behind me to pay attention to some nerd getting brave inside a fucking Toyota. Bet the little douche wouldn't be doing shit if we were face-to-face somewhere.

There's a loud *pop* and I floor it. The fuck's shooting at us, I know it. I hope Avery puts that Glock to use and rings his ass back. Maybe he'll wreck or something and I can lose him enough to get to the club in one piece.

"It was a tire, on a car back there. It went out." Avery screams loudly so I can hear her over the roar of my engine and the wind.

Looking in the side mirror I watch as a car pulls off to the side. She must be right and it's the best fucking thing for us. It screwed up traffic enough that the Snake's stuck trying to get through the cluster.

This area is horrible for accidents, especially with the never ending road construction going on. There seems to be someone in a wreck or getting a flat every time I ride on it as well. Granted, that's not much, but still. I'm going to take every advantage of this right now.

I hit the next exit and take the back farm road to the connecting road that leads to the club. It's dusty and bumpy, so we only ride on it for secret runs or we all know to use it for an emergency as well. In this situation, I need to get to the club quick, so I have to use it.

Avery squeaks occasionally whenever we hit a bump, but she's been a trooper so far. She's surprised the hell out of me to be honest. I'm going to have to check my girl out tomorrow — poor bike. She ain't good for this kind of shit. Avery's probably going to be sore as fuck from holding on and all the bumps as well.

Fuck, Prez is going to flip the fuck out when he hears about this shit too. Cain will go ballistic if he thinks London and Jamison will be in any danger too. That guy's like a damn grizzly bear when it comes to his family.

Shit, I can feel Avery shaking like crazy behind me. I bet she's scared out of her mind.

"It's okay, Shorty, we'll be there in a few minutes and you can lie down and relax." I reach back to rest my hand on her thigh. "You good?"

"Umm," she groans and shakes even worse.

"Avery? What's going on? Talk to me." I squeeze her leg a few times but she remains quiet. "Yo, babe, the fuck?"

She begins to sob into the back of my cut and buries her head into the leather. I stop questioning her, concentrating on the ride and getting to the club as soon as possible. I can't believe this shit happened while she was with me. It angers me that the asshole was shooting at me, but to do it and threaten Avery? It makes me fucking boil inside.

We arrive at the club about five minutes later. My baby's shaken up and probably won't walk well after such a rough ride. "Hey, Shorty, let me get off first, you'll probably be a little wobbly."

She keeps quiet and I scrunch my forehead. I know it was scary for her, but if she can't handle that little bit, she won't be able to handle this life.

I get off the bike, taking in the parking lot. Looks like everyone made it home and we have a full house. Cain's Challenger is here so that means London and the baby are here too.

I turn to help Avery climb down. She's ghostly pale and her lip's trembling. "Free bird. It's not so bad, come here." I'll hold her until she calms, my poor woman.

"I've-I-I've been s-shot," she whispers as tears trail down her already tear-stained face.

Scanning over her body, I desperately scan every inch of her. She glances down to her leg and I notice blood oozing out of the side of her thigh.

Fuck! I look at my hand that was just holding her leg and sure enough, it's covered in blood. How in the fuck did I not notice this? It had to be the adrenaline, to make me so oblivious to the wetness coating my palm.

Pulling her to my chest, I her into my arms and carry her as quickly as possible towards the clubhouse.

"It's okay, Avery. Everything will be fine, I'll look you over as soon as we get inside and I'll fix it. I'll fix this; I promise I can make it better. I promise, okay?" I ramble, scatterbrained at her being injured.

This should've happened to me- me. Not her.

The main door flies open and Niko exits onto the platform in front of the door. His eyes grow wide when he sees us and he scurries down the four stairs with his hands out to grab Avery.

"Give me her," he demands.

"No fuckin' way, Niko, get out of my way, now." I bark and attempt to weave my way around him.

"You fuck! Give her to me now," he shouts, panic echoing through his heavy Russian accent.

"Back the fuck up, Niko. I ain't muthafuckin' playing right now. Get out of my way." I slam into his shoulder, attempting to head for the door again.

"No, you give her. I transport upstairs and you retrieve supplies."

Well, now that makes sense to me. I nod, begrudgingly and tenderly place her into his arms. She wraps her hands around his neck and gives him a sad smile.

It pulls at my heartstrings to see her so welcoming and comfortable with him. I know he's good to her and they have fun, but it doesn't mean I have to like it. I can't believe this just happened to her.

That pop didn't sound like a damn car tire blowing; I should've pulled over and checked on her when we got on the farm road. She was shaking so badly, I should've realized it was more than her being scared.

She appears so weak and disheveled. I can't stand that look on my fierce woman; she's normally stubborn and full of life. I have to fix her leg so she feels better, then I have to shower her in attention.

I jog in front of Niko and up the stairs, yanking the door open. I pull it as far as it will go, giving them room to get through the door easily.

As soon as the door opens, music pours out. "Hurry up, fucker, so I can get her cleaned up." I gesture dramatically toward the doorway.

"Don't you hurry me, you imbecile. This is your fault. She with me, she does not return shot and wounded," he grits heatedly. I glower at him as he passes me on his way into the club.

"Set her on the couch and yell for the Prez. I'm going to get the supplies to check her leg out." I run to the bathroom to get the medical bag.

I don't want her to be uncomfortable. Christ, all a sudden I've turned into the fucking club doctor or something. I guess it's just in my nature to want to take care of people, after taking care of Sadie for so long.

"Brother." Ares nods and grumbles while he takes a piss.

I glance up at him, unaware he was even in here with me. I'm focused strictly on Avery and no one else. I nod back and rush to the closet, ripping all the supplies I may need off the shelf.

Towels, I need towels.

Toilet paper rolls and paper towels go flying everywhere onto the floor as I shove stuff out of my way. Ares watches me as if I've gone mad. I have gone mad though.

Once I get my girl cleaned up and taken care of, that ghostly-looking motherfucker is mine. Make my girl bleed? It's fucking on. I'll ride out with Nightmare and Exterminator if I have to. I know Nikoli will take care of Avery while I handle business.

This is two hits against the club; brothers won't stand for it. Avery and Brently aren't members, but Brently is family and Avery is with me now. She may not know it yet, but it will happen.

I need to let Prez know I'm laying claim. If anything, so I get retribution for this today. She never deserved this shit happening to her.

Ares watches my frantic pace and finally notices the blood on my shirt when I turn toward him. "Shit, man, who's hurt? What happened?" He stares at me, full of surprise and concern.

"I was followed at the store by a Twisted Snake and Avery was shot on the way home. I'll explain it all to you guys later. I need to get to her."

He nods, quickly moving out of my way and I head toward the bathroom counter, laying the supplies on the large surface. "Yeah, brother, of course, go to her."

I wash my hands well in the bathroom sink then snatch up my supplies and make my way back to Avery. It's not sterile, but it's better than nothing. I know that nasty fucking couch will be the most unsanitary out of everything. There's no telling who's fucked and what not on it.

Ares follows and when I see her, she's lying unmoving and pale. She looks weak and broken. Nikoli, Prez, Cain, Twist, and Nightmare all surround the couch watching her, waiting for me. I'm sure they're wondering what the fuck a chick is doing on our couch, bleeding, with a pissed off Russian standing guard next to her.

I kneel and place all my items on the table and turn to Avery to cut a hole in her pants and get to her wound.

"2? Explain, brother," Prez booms. He's standing, gazing at me sternly, waiting for me to say the word. Fuck, he's pissed. I'm sure he has a good idea of what went down and wants confirmation so he can handle it like he's been waiting to.

"I will, Prez. Let me cut this first."

Keeping my focus on the shredded material from the bullet, I pull out my knife and slice a hole in her pants. Ripping the rest of the material from under her leg, I tug the bottom portion of her pants leg down.

I start dumping rubbing alcohol on her thigh, patting it lightly, so I can see what's going on and just how serious this is. If it's bad, I'll call the real doctor straight away. I'm done fucking around; I'll make sure that this time she's properly taken care of.

"They were followed, Prez. by a fucking Snake. Guess he shot Avery," Ares grumbles to the guys next to me.

Prez turns bright red and looks like his head may pop off. "What?" he explodes pissed off. "Are you fucking kidding me right now with this?" he shouts, his gaze flying to me.

I nod with a somber look.

"Nah, Prez. I'm not fucking around," I recant the events from the store up until we pulled into the parking lot and I discovered Avery had been shot.

"She need the doc?" he gestures toward Avery.

"No, it's not too bad. The shot hit toward the outside of her leg, straight through. I'm going to clean it out good then sew it up." I glance back at Avery and see her watching me silently.

She's not even crying anymore, she just looks exhausted. "I'm so sorry, Shorty."

"I know." She turns her face away, toward the black leather cushion and closes her eyes. I fucked up bad this time. I never should've had her in that situation in the first place.

"Will someone get her some Jack?" I look around at the brothers.

Ares straightens up, "Yeah, brother. No problem." He walks behind the bar and grabs her a fresh bottle of Jack Daniels.

128

Good. After she takes a sip, I need to drink about half of that shit myself. He hands me the bottle and I nod in appreciation.

"This fucking shit has to stop and now. I want each one of those Snakes. I want them to fucking hurt. They come rolling up, fucking with people in my club? Not happening. I want this handled ASAP, no more pussy-footing around, Ares." Prez orders and cracks his knuckles.

Twist looks crazed, his face radiating anger. He nods profusely at Prez. "I want to go, Prez," he snickers. "I have something good for them." He grins, evil filling his gaze.

Prez affirms, nodding, "Yes, I'll send a few of our roughest to clean house, fucking chop the heads off all those fucking slimy bastards. Enough, this gets discussed in church."

I turn back to Avery. She drinks straight from the bottle, swallowing a big gulp. Normally, I'd give her major props for that shit, but right now is not the time to tease her and give her grief.

I pat her wound again and glance up at her. "You ready, free bird? I stalled to give you a little time for that Jack to play its part. I know it's going to hurt, but I'll move as fast as I can baby, I promise. I don't want to hurt you."

"Yes, just get it over with please. I can't stand to see my own blood; that's why I almost passed out earlier. It freaks me out. Other people's blood I'm okay with, but not mine."

Yeah, the Jack has kicked in, because my girl is talking a little more normal now.

"Come on, biker. You either fix it or I take her to doctor." Niko glowers at me and I curl my lip.

"I'm fixing it, *RUSSIAN*, just trying to make sure it doesn't hurt her as much. Let the alcohol work its magic," I reply shortly and turn back to her leg.

"Yeah, man, back the fuck off my brother. He was just shot at too and doesn't need your fuckin' bullshit," Twist gripes to Niko.

"Hey, easy now. Twist, back the fuck up yourself and go tell the brothers that church is in an hour," Prez cuts in, before it can turn really ugly and we end up with a dead Niko.

Nightmare stands solemn and silent the entire time, watching and waiting before he ever speaks or makes a move. Twist turns, looking peeved and heads for the other brothers. I wonder where London is. I can't believe she hasn't come in here to chew my head off already for getting Avery hurt.

"Hey, man, saw Loretta parked out front, where's your ol' lady and kid?" I glance to Cain briefly then back at my work.

He chuckles. "Why, you scared that she's going to scalp your ass for Avery getting injured?"

"She should — or I could — I have knife," Niko suggests and smiles at Cain.

"Nah, man, don't fuck with 2; he'd never do anything to get Avery hurt purposefully."

Niko rolls his eyes and huffs off to the bar, probably for his beloved vodka.

"London and my boy are at home. Ares needed to use my truck, so I brought Loretta along. She needed a good wash," he replies fondly.

He and Ares must've had fun with some poor idiot. He's going to make a good Enforcer with Ares someday. Brother keeps it up like he is and he'll be voted Enforcer before he knows it. Ares would be happy to have permanent help too.

I nod while Nightmare just stands next to Prez watching me. It's kind of creepy, but he does have a pretty fucked up name and a scar running over one of his eyes.

Avery has hers closed tightly. Poor Shorty, I'm such a failure at keeping her from getting hurt one way or another.

"All right, baby, all done. I'm going to need to carry you to the bed, so you can rest and relax though. It's all covered up with gauze and tape, so you can look. It shouldn't make you sick."

I stand and stretch my muscles. "Prez, Nightmare, I'm going to go and get her settled in, I'll be back in a while to discuss this with y'all." Nightmare stares at me and doesn't say anything, go figure,

Prez nods and glances sympathetically at Avery. "Church in an hour," he grunts.

"I'll be there," I confirm and scoop Avery into my arms carefully.

"Ouch!" she groans into my neck.

"Sorry, Shorty, just have to get a good grip on you. I got you, okay?"

She nods against my throat and grips me tighter. Ares follows us and opens my room door so I don't jostle her any more.

"Thanks, brother."

"No problem. Angel, if you need anything, just holler, baby," he mumbles to her, it sounding a bit gruff. He's a broody bastard like Nightmare.

"Okay, thank you, Ares." She sends him a pained smile and he shuts door as he leaves.

I lay her down gradually, attempting to make the transition somewhat gentle from my arms to the bed. Next, I take her socks and shoes off, rubbing her ankles and arches as I go. Anything I can do for her, I will.

"Are you comfy, free bird? You need me to move the pillows around or get you something else to drink?" I mutter and slowly lie down beside her on the bed, attempting to be careful and not shake her or cause any unwanted movements that'll bring her more discomfort.

"No, thanks, I'm not an invalid you know. Blood just makes me squeamish. I'm not nauseous anymore, though. However, the bullet did hurt pretty badly when it hit. I thought something had burned me, until I realized what had happened. When I saw all the blood, I had to keep quiet or I would've either puked or conked out. I figured silence was better than hitting the dirt," she explains and rubs her petite palm over my scruffy cheek.

I relish the feeling; it's comforting and relaxes me enough to make me sleepy. I turn in to her touch and squeeze my eyes closed for a few beats.

"Fuck, I'm sorry, baby. This never should've happened. You shouldn't be mixed up with me and this club shit. I don't want you to get hurt or worse, dead."

"Look, 2, I'm a big girl, okay? I can handle when times aren't easy. It was the blood; otherwise, I'm perfectly fine."

I stare at her incredulously. "You mean to tell me, you're not flipping out in that head of yours? Not even a smidge about getting shot, someone chasing us on my bike, and then me sewing you up?"

"No, I'm not. It was crazy and I got one hell of an adrenaline rush, but I'm okay now. I panicked at first but then I got over it. I was honestly so busy worrying that something would happen and you'd be hurt. I stopped having time to panic with all of the stuff going on."

"I'm finding that a little hard to believe. I've been at this shit a whole minute. Stuff just happened, and you're already cool. Nah, Shorty that sort still gets my heart pumping." I shake my head in disbelief.

No way can she be so calm about it. I wonder how she'd react seeing me take my Glocks out and shooting some fucker dead right in front of her. Would she still blame it on the blood, or give in and admit that club life can be fucked up?

I know it inside, hell, we all know that our way of life is fucked up in many ways. There are many of us who're screwed up though and this life calls to us. We have an innate need for freedom, a wildness that runs rampant in our veins.

She shrugs. "Look, you can believe and feel however you want. I knew about Tate before anyone else and it didn't bother me one bit. I just asked that the Mafia please not come after me since I knew about them. Niko handles some crazy stuff, but who am I to judge what he does without me? You're the same way; I'm aware you don't play cards with the boys and keep everything G-rated. You do what is expected from you and what you enjoy. As long as I am treated well, then I couldn't care less what you get into in your free time. Like you said before, that's club business, which means it's not my business."

I'm a little impressed and surprised with her response and reasoning. Could I really have a girl who can understand my way of life, maybe even enjoy it? I'm almost too scared to hope, but can't help myself.

"I'm glad you look at it that way, Shorty. Speaking of, I have to get to church and check in with my brothers." I kiss her affectionately on the tip of her nose and stand. "You need something before I split?"

"No, thanks, I'm okay. I'm going to hang out here and try to take a nap. I'm worn out after all that madness earlier."

I nod and make my way to church, giving her some peace.

Niko's still sitting at the bar looking angry.

"Hey, Nikoli, she's chilling in my room. She said she's going to take a nap, but she'd probably want to see you beforehand."

He regards me with raised his eyebrows, "Good, I'll check on her," He grumbles, shortly.

Well, you're welcome, asshole.

Now, to find out what Prez's plan is, and defile some scum.

Avery

There's a sharp burn radiating up my thigh and it hurts so fucking bad. *It was a skim.* I don't give a shit if it was a skim or in the gut; this damn hole is painful.

I was trying so hard to be brave in front of everyone. I wanted to cry and hide my face so no one could see how bad it affected me. I've never been hurt before doing anything like that, so I don't have a high pain tolerance.

Maybe I should get a couple of tattoos to help me build it up, especially if I have to worry about this sort of thing taking place.

I can't believe 2's doubting me. I may not be around his type of lifestyle on the regular, or ever to be realistic, but still. I wish he would have a touch of faith in me.

I'm still here; I haven't run off scared yet. I was aware getting involved with a biker could bring complications. I didn't think they'd affect me though. I can handle it. He may not have faith in me right now, but I believe in myself.

My head's still spinning with the fact he just sewed up my cut. I mean, who does that?

Oh, you're shot, let's just sew you up like new and you'll be fine. It's just a skim.

I wanted to throat punch him when he said it's just a skim. Leave it to me to move from a Mafia man to a biker. At least here they seem to take care of their own and there's a strong sense of loyalty.

Those Mafia guys will kill their own wives if they have to. Not Tate and Emily, but others would. I really hope I'm never on the receiving end of their wrath.

To think, I could be at the coffee shop right this moment. I'd be serving fru-fru drinks to men in suits and questioning my reasons for being there. Instead, I'm laid up in a biker compound, shot in the leg. Why am I not surprised in the least?

Maybe I should call my mom. I'd relish the fact this situation would drive her berserk. My dad would probably laugh until I got to telling him the details of being shot.

I'm still creeped out by the scary-looking guy who was following us around the store too. He looked flat out malicious. I thought Spin was scary back when the guys were fighting, but this other guy made Spin look like a freaking boy scout.

I wonder how Brently is doing healing up and that awful tattoo. Spin's going to have to ink all of Brently's stomach to attempt to cover up that nasty gouged in lettering. It reminds me of someone taking an apple peeler and trying to tattoo with it. The letters are big, chunky, black, and appear scribbled.

I don't know how he made it through it; I would've passed out. It makes me nauseous just thinking about it. I heard Brently talking this past week about how he's thinking of prospecting for the Oath Keepers now. I'm guessing being a badass is looking better to him, especially after his experience with that other club.

The guys keep quiet about their business stuff, but I've caught little bits and pieces from different members. I think Ares is my favorite out of them so far. Most of the guys are standoffish but Ares speaks to me sometimes. He's broody and grumbles a lot, but he's also sexy as hell and smart. I thought he was a huge jerk-off, but he's quite the opposite once you get to know him a little.

I can understand how London fit into this life so easily. It's freeing here. You don't worry about the everyday mundane bullshit. Everyone at the club pitches in and enjoys each other's company, to where it reminds me of a giant family. I hope the others warm up to me like Ares has eventually.

I think back to how sweet he was the other day…

Two days prior…

"Hey, Avery, can I borrow you a sec?" he grumbles, appearing peeved.

I glance over at him, confused, wondering what he could possibly have to say to me. The other night was awkward enough. I really don't know if I can talk to him without blushing like a schoolgirl after being a prude and locking myself into the bathroom.

I tilt my lips into a miniscule grin and nod. Probably better to say as little as possible; I don't want to come off as a complete hot mess to this beautiful man.

He nods back and heads for a small table toward the back of the room. I always see him sitting at the same spot in the bar area, nearly at the same time daily too. "Sit, please." He gestures to the opposite seat.

Swallowing, I do as he asks. "Okay, sure." I sit and stare at my hands on the table top, playing with my nails.

I have no clue what on Earth to say. I'm so embarrassed to be sitting in front of him like this. *Please don't bring up the other day, please.*

"So, I wanted to get with you about the other day."

Damn it. Obviously, this day is working against me and not with me. I keep my gaze trained on my nails hoping I'll disappear suddenly and reappear on a nice beach somewhere. You ever wonder if you sit still long enough, whether maybe you can just blend in? Well, that's what I'm going for right now.

Bang!

His fist slams on the table and I jump. The glass and bottle rattle; making me wince and clench my stomach. I'm just counting the seconds until it falls and shatters.

He snatches them quickly, silencing the ruckus. Then he covers my fingers with one of his huge, strong hands, breaking my trance. "Am I so ugly that you don't want to look me in the face?" he snarls angrily.

What the hell is he talking about? I glance up and am met with his harsh stare.

"Well?"

"Um, no. Not at all, the opposite actually. I'm a little embarrassed about the other day."

God, is he crazy? He's built like a goddamn Spartan warrior and he believes I don't want to look at him. I'm still kicking myself for not licking every inch of his expansive chest when I had the chance.

"That's what I wanted to talk about," he mutters, calmer now, and his voice makes me clench my core.

"Okay."

He stares at me perplexed. "Okay?"

"Yep, okay," I reply meeting his gaze. I can do this one word thing all day, if he'd like.

"Yeah, so I talked to 2 about what went down. He told me you thought you were going to be passed around."

I nod and lay my hands flat on the sticky table.

He shakes his head. "It's not like that. I'd never hurt you. I may be a controlling bastard and enjoy some wicked shit, but I'd never put it on you, if that's not your thing."

"Thank you for saying that, I know that now. It was just overwhelming at the time and I didn't know what to do or how to act. I should've stayed and talked it out with you guys. I tend to get dramatic sometimes and clam up."

"I can see it being overwhelming and shit. Anyhow, I'm sorry," he admits and stares at my fingers, massaging my hands softly.

I really don't want to speak and break this moment, whatever's happening, but I have to say something. "I mean...I totally would've, you know. If I'd have known what was going on."

His head shoots up, meeting my eyes again, surprise clearly written on his features. "Yeah?"

"Yes, definitely. I'd be crazy not to take advantage of that situation," I whisper, and he grins roguishly.

"We may be able to work somethin' out in the future." He chuckles and my mouth tips into a smile.

I feel like my heart may beat out of my chest. "Maybe, if you're lucky," I quip smoothly and he laughs a little louder.

"Guess we'll just have to wait and see then, huh?"

"Guess so." I flirt, wearing a wide smile.

Who knew Ares could play or be sweet or be the first to mend fences?

God, I never would've guessed in a million years that Ares and I would've had that conversation. Ever since that chat, he gets a mischievous grin on his face whenever I walk past him. 2 Piece thought he was weird until I told him about the discussion we had. Now, 2 rolls his eyes and chuckles when he sees Ares grinning at me. I don't understand why he gets so jealous over my friendship with Niko, but is okay if I'm flirty with Ares.

Men are weird; I'll never understand them. Nikoli and I have a past together, but that ship has sailed. We're only good friends now. No, scratch that; we're best friends.

I love him like a super-sized, hot, blond stepbrother, not as a fuck buddy anymore. I wish I could convince 2 that he has zero competition in that department. He could have all of me if he wanted to, but he's not at that level. I want that with him though; I want everything. If anything, experiencing things like today makes me open to live in the moment even more.

There's a knock and I glance up as it opens. "Bean?" Nikoli call as he pokes his head through the crack.

"Hey, Niko, come in," I croak and he scrunches his brow. "I'm okay, just thirsty." I take a big drink of my bottled water and clear my throat. "There, see, much better. I think my throat is a little sore from screaming at 2 over the bike's engine earlier."

"Doesn't make it any better. Ass is in doghouse with me," he grits in a snarky tone.

"Ugh, Niko, why? I don't understand; why don't you guys just get along?" I sigh, exasperated.

"Because he is not good enough for my Bean," he admits in his deep Russian accent.

Aw, that is so sweet. At the same time, though, it's very frustrating. I love the fact he cares so much for me. I'd be protective of him, too, if the situation were reversed.

The difference is that 2 Piece can protect me himself. He did so earlier, by getting me out of the store quickly and his crazy weaving in and out of traffic. He could've easily given me over to the creepy guy and let him do whatever he wanted to. Instead, he did his best to protect me and get me back to safety.

143

"Thank you, Niko, but maybe I'm not good enough for him? There's so much more to him than you realize."

For example, he's considerate. He takes care of others and it doesn't even faze him. It's like second nature, and I'm sure he doesn't realize he's doing it most of the time.

"Humph," Niko grunts, and lies back onto the bed beside me.

He's so large that the covers pull tightly and squish me with his weight. His feet dangle off the end of the bed and I grin up at him. "You do not understand. In Russia, it is the man's job to not let girl get hurt. He let you get shot, so his fault." He shrugs like it's the simplest thing to understand.

I rake my fingers through Nikoli's soft blond hair and he closes his eyes. Whoever ends up winning this man is going to have a fierce protector. She'll be one lucky lady. Well, aside from the scary Mafia stuff I'm sure he deals with that I'm not privy to.

"But he did protect me. He left the store and brought me back here as fast as he could. He didn't know the guy was going to shoot me. He even had a gun to put in his boot."

"That is no excuse. Why not use the gun, then?" He opens his eyes and gazes at me earnestly, interrupting what I was saying.

"I was the stubborn one and told him to let me hold it for him. He took it back when we parked the bike. I was lucky I was able to even hold on to it and him." I raise my voice arguing and he snarls.

144

"See that's it, another thing. He ride bike and you can fall off."

"You're just being ornery now. You know I love riding on motorcycles. Don't start trying to boss me like my parents always do. I'm twenty-three years old for Christ's sake. I can make my own decisions. I love you, Niko, I really do, but I can't deal with this. I'm starting to fall for him and his ways. I need your support."

"You always have my support, Bean, you know I love you," he whispers, his eyes softening towards me.

"I know, just, please stop fighting with him. You arguing and stuff is not supporting me. I miss my fun Niko. You've been so serious since we got here. What's going on?"

"I am still fun Niko, this is business. I told you not to come. I knew I would be tired and grouch."

I giggle a little at his wording.

"Well, stop being grouchy. I'm already here, so there's nothing we can do about it now."

"Yes, I take you home and keep you safe, like good Russian man," he declares, nodding to himself.

"I mean it, stop. You're pissing me off. I'm not going anywhere, I'm staying with 2."

"Oh yeah? You stay now or forever?"

"Good question. I guess we'll have to see." I shrug and he rolls his eyes.

"I hope you know what you are doing. I will back off, but I think you are being stupid right now."

"Gee, please tell me how you really feel."

"I do."

"I know, Niko, I know."

"Okay, if you stay here, I am going back to the hotel. I know the bikers will be up to something soon now and I need to rest prior."

"Okay, be careful," I warn, and he kisses me on my cheek.

Right before he leaves he blows me a kiss and I smile. He's always done. I used to think it was romantic, but now I know it's just because he's sweet. I've never seen him do it to any of the other girls though, and that makes me feel special.

My phone makes its signature bubble sound and I check the incoming text. It's from London. I wonder if Cain told her what had happened.

London: Hey hootchie mama, you okay?

Me: Hi. Yes, fine, just a scratch. Cain tell you?

London: Yes, you know this. Would you like to come back to the house?

Me: No, I'm just going to stay here. 2's taking care of me.

London: I bet he is! LOL. Okay I hope you get better soon and if you change your mind, we'll come get you. I

called to tell Em, but they're out of the country on vacation. Tate wanted to surprise her before she's too far along to travel. Her cell reception was shit, so she told me to let you know she loves you. I didn't tell her you were shot, just that she should give you a call sometime when she had a chance. I didn't want to worry her and Tate.

Me: All right, thank you. I appreciate it and I'll give you a shout if I need to be busted out of here.

London: Sure thing lady.

Me: Later.

I got lucky meeting Emily when she moved to Tennessee. That girl thought she was going to sit in the back of that lecture hall, all isolated. She didn't know it, but I was all by myself too and lonely. I've met many people over the years, but none of them really stuck to me.

I love Emily like a sister, and without her I never would've met London, Nikoli, and 2 Piece. I love London to pieces too; she's so fun and goofy. Tate's not so bad either. He isn't close to anyone but Niko however. I still wonder what happened with the whole Cameron situation.

I'm happy Emily and Tate found each other. They've both been through so much; they deserve to be happy. I can't believe Emily overcame everything she did. I don't think she ever had a chance though. Tate took one look at her and made it his mission to save her.

She was crazy thinking she could keep everything bottled up to deal with single-handedly, and that we all weren't going to help her. Thank God for Tate manning up and embracing his Russian background he kept trying to hide from. Now he's the Big Boss. I never would've guessed that was going to happen.

I can only hope to be half the person Emily has grown to become. She genuinely thinks and cares about everyone else but herself. She's going to make a wonderful mother, and Tate will make a great, loving father.

I'm getting sleepy and I wish 2 was in here taking care of me, but he's in church handling his club stuff. They'll eventually go after these guys. The President said as much when they were stitching up my leg. It's amazing what people will say when they think you aren't paying any attention.

I just hope 2 Piece doesn't get hurt. I feel like I'm just getting to know him and have barely found him. I don't want to have to let him go already.

A door slams and I'm jolted out of my peaceful slumber. I must've dozed off. I shift and there's this hulking dark shadow at the end of the bed.

"2? Baby, is that you?" I whisper drowsily. My vision's a little blurry and I swear that shadow looks bigger than the one I've gotten used to.

"No, it's me. 2's on his way," he mumbles and takes his shirt off.

I make out the outline of his shredded torso in the moonlight streaming through the blinds. He flips the leather through his belt buckle with skillful fingers, unbuttoning his jeans next. His pants remain propped up on his sharply defined hips and thick muscular thighs. The image of him like this makes me gulp, my eyes growing wide.

"O-oh, okay. Are you staying in here tonight or something?"

I swallow and take a drink of my water waiting on the bedside table. I need to wake up and make sure I'm seriously having this conversation right now. This could be one hell of a good dream.

"Or something." He shrugs and pushes his pants down. His hefty, straining cock pops out and bobs a little with it's girth.

Damn, commando.

The bedroom door opens and I know I must be caught gaping when 2 Piece steps in. "You getting Shorty warmed up yet?" 2 grins and peers at him. He shuts the door and the light behind him disappears with it.

"About to," he rumbles, and I feel myself start to get wet.

I have little zings deep inside my pussy just watching them both standing here like this. He comes closer to the bed, ordering, "Spread your legs, I want a taste."

"'Kay," I squeak, doing as I'm told.

2 chuckles, tugging his shirt free while he watches. He pops his pants button but doesn't move to take them off.

There's a ripping sound and my gaze shoots down to my panties. He's ripping them free like a piece of birthday ribbon. They're in shreds, outright ruined, but I couldn't care less right now.

Breaths leave my mouth quicker, nearly panting, as his face leans close to my core. He grabs my thigh that isn't injured and shoves it up toward my stomach and then dives straight in to sucking my clit. I turn to 2 wide-eyed with my mouth gaping open.

"Holy fuck! Ares, God!" I gasp, moaning loudly and 2 shoves his pants down.

His dick strains against his boxer briefs, begging to be let out to play. His irises darken as he watches Ares go to work. His hand finds the hard length, stroking over the material at the sight of us.

Ares sticks a long finger in my pussy and I clench around it. He releases a breathy groan into my center. Little vibrations run through me and I soak his hand with my spasms.

2 steps to the bed, planting one knee onto the mattress, ready to join in. He moves toward me swiftly, dips his head to my breast, and draws the tip through his thin white T-shirt I'd borrowed. My nipple puckers at the wet material and the scratchy sensation creates a wonderful friction.

"Fuck," I moan and grip their hair in each of my hands.

2 pulls away, his face flushed and his eyes tell me he's ready to ravish me. He removes my shirt, staring his fill.

I'm lying here completely naked and vulnerable in front of two beautiful men. One looks as if he was meant to be in Spartacus and the other like the bad boy your momma warned you about while growing up. I'm in awe and can't wait to sample them together.

Ares pulls his finger out of me and replaces it with his tongue. His sweet, blissful mouth taking it's fill, while giving me pleasure.

2 dips back down to taste and nibble on my right breast. Ares moves, licking and kissing up my torso until each of them have a mouthful of my breasts.

Fuck, it's like heaven, to feel each tongue swirling, their mouths nipping and biting on my erect nipples, the caresses and rough hands. It's too much, and my pussy clenches, begging for relief.

"Please," I beg breathlessly, not above pleading if I have to.

Ares reaches below, pushing two fingers into my hot, wet core.

At the same time 2 caresses me, scooping some of my pussy juice onto his finger tips and then sticks them in my ass. The stretch and burn, the little zings of pain and pleasure have me igniting and exploding like nothing I've ever felt before. My pussy floods with wetness, making me moan incoherent ramblings through my pleasure. I stop coming and they both sit back.

Ares watches me while I take a few deep breaths, trying to regain my composure.

2 Piece rubs his hand gently down my side and gives me a small smile. "You okay, Shorty?"

I nod my head. I'm incapable of speaking at the moment. They just rocked my world and they only used their mouths and tongues to do it. I will just say right now, there is nothing like two men at one time with their mouths on you. *Holy fucking shit balls.* I could kick myself now for not allowing this to happen sooner.

Ares grabs my hand, kissing it tenderly and I melt a bit. He's wearing the sweetest expression I've seen from him before.

I give him a reassuring smile. I want him to know I'm okay with this and that I loved what just happened.

2 caresses my face and Ares lays over, rubbing his fingers through my hair. It's so relaxing, I feel cherished and pampered. The liquor from earlier still thrums through my

body; making my body and mind more comfortable and accepting of them both staring—taking me in.

I'm just going to close my eyes for a minute.

At least that's what I tell myself as sleep and exhaustion overcomes me.

2 Piece

"Wake her up," Ares grins mischievously.

"Fuck no; I'm not waking her up. She was shot today. If we aren't careful, she'll get skittish and leave." I'm going to do everything in my power to make sure she's comfortable and happy. It's the least she deserves after all the bullshit.

"Brother, my dick is hard as granite and that—just a few minutes ago—was hot as fuck."

"Shh. You're going to wake her up. It'll happen, just give it some time. What we just showed her was perfect, she'll want more," I whisper and glare at his stubborn ass. If he wakes her up on purpose or by accident—doesn't matter—I'm going to be pissed either way.

"Fine," he huffs and starts getting dressed. "Make sure she's okay in the morning, I don't want her freaked out like she was the last time we tried to have fun with her. I like this one and she's responsive to us both."

"She'll be fine. I'll talk to her in the morning in case she's tripping out." He nods and we fist bump on his way out.

Pulling the covers back, I take her in. She's so sensual, with her hair spread out on the pillow behind her. She's peaceful with her hand tucked under the pillow beside her face.

Her tits are swollen and have little bites on them, proof of our fun. Following along the line of her smooth stomach, my eyes pause on her bare pussy lips next. *Fuck, I want her bad.*

I keep observing and get to the big white bandage on the side of her thigh. *I can't believe that shit happened. Damn it.*

I have to get that piece of shit who hurt her. I'll talk with the brothers more about it tomorrow to finalize the plans we made in church and to let Nikoli in on everything. It will be dealt with, that I promise.

Crawling into bed beside her, I'm careful not to rouse her too much with the dip I create in the mattress. Fixing the covers around her, I lay my hand over her waist. I want her to be comfortable but still be able to hold her while I sleep.

Taking a deep breath, I can't help but think about how much I want the woman lying beside me, as I join her in blissful sleep.

I wake up to Avery's warm body sprawled all over me. She has her bad leg propped on top of mine and her arms wrapped around me like a little spider monkey. Closing my eyes, I relish the feeling for a few seconds. We haven't gotten many moments like this during her visit. Normally there isn't much going on when she's here, so we can hang around and chill with each other.

My eyes pop open at the pounding coming from my door. That must be the reason I woke up in the first place.

"Wakey, wakey, printyessas," Nikoli calls from the other side.

Fucking dick.

He's going to wake Avery and she needs a lot of rest. I don't want her up and hurting or questioning shit.

There's more booming from him banging on the door. And I swear I'm going to punch that fucker again. I have a nice bruise on my cheek from his big-ass knuckles, but I'll have the element of surprise this time.

Relinquish

I ease my way out from under her. It's kind of hard with the grip she has on my hip though.

"Errm." She stirs and I could kick that idiot for waking me up.

"Shh, baby, I'm going to the bathroom."

I don't know why I didn't just tell her Niko's at the door, maybe because I know she'll let him in. I don't want him in here when she's lying naked in my bed. He may've seen her like this before, but not while I have her. She's not actually mine, but I'm beginning to work on changing that.

Creeping over to open the door quietly, I'm met with a cheery and bright eyed Russian asshole. "'Sup, biker, how was the night?"

"Shh, man, fuck. Shorty's sleeping and she needs her rest."

"Why, what's wrong with her?" he grumbles angrily, glaring.

"Nothing's wrong; she had a rough day yesterday and I want her to get the rest she needs."

"Good, that is understandable."

"Why are you banging on my door, anyhow?"

"I believe your Prez has told you to tell me plan, yes?" his accent heavy. .

"All right, hold up a minute. Let me get my pants." I shut the door and put on last night's jeans, a clean, black T-

156

shirt and my cut. Then I run my hands through my hair, but there's not much there to worry about in the first place.

Ugh, my body's stiff.

I need to go work out; it's been two days and I can tell the difference. Cain has a family now and still makes time to work out pretty much daily. I need to make it a priority again. I've been good about it this last week, but I need to become more devoted to it like he is.

I'm more the outside type to exercise anyhow; if it's not too hot, that is. Here in Texas that's only like three months out of the year. I enjoy doing manual labor and working out with the big ropes and tractor tires we have out back.

Slipping on my motorcycle boots over a fresh pair of socks, I check for my wallet. It's still in my back pocket attached to my chain, so I'm straight. Hopefully, Avery's still asleep.

"Okay, let's go into the main room or the bar." I mutter when I get back to the hall.

"As you wish."

I follow as he heads toward the bar. "I need coffee first off. You want any?"

"No, I only like *Bean's* coffee."

"Yep, she's good at that, huh," I grunt gruffly. I wonder what else he likes about her. *Bean?* Who the fuck calls someone *Bean,* anyhow?

"Yes," he says simply, and I check out his shirt as I come around the bar. It reads *FBI, female body inspector.*

"Humph," I huff as I pass him and take a seat with a stool between us.

"No more bad blood between us, 2 Piece."

"Oh yeah, how do you figure?" I mutter with a touch of hostility.

"Avery ask to back off you, so I agree. I do not mean to stand in your way. You could be her future. She cares for you, so I step back and be friendly."

Great, he's going to make me look like the asshole in this now. He was the dick first off by fighting with me, but now he plans to redeem himself it seems.

"How do I know if you're genuine? You could be fake as fuck right now and bad mouthing me when you have her alone."

He looks at me with confusion and annoyance.

"Look, I just call it like I see it," I shrug, taking a large gulp of coffee and damn near burn my tongue off. I choke that shit down though. I won't lo weak in any aspect in front of this blond-haired brute.

"I'm here to help you and to protect Avery. I have no reason to be misleading. I will simply say what I think to your face. Clearly I am not scared of you." He nods toward my cheek where I have a dark bruise from the fight we got into.

Dick.

"Yes, and clearly, I'm not scared of your ass either," I nod toward his forehead. It's where the cut is right above his eyebrow, from one of my punches. I may not be the biggest guy around, but I'm not going to let anyone think they intimidate me. It's probably stupid. I know Nikoli could most likely kick my ass. Being in the club life, though, you learn to stand up for yourself and not take any shit.

"Very good. Then we move past. I won't speak of it again."

I nod again, accepting the mutually agreed on terms. I catch him talking shit and stirring up drama with me and Shorty, then it's on like fucking Donkey Kong.

"Yeah, cool. All right, so business. Prez has a plan. It's going to entail Ares, Cain, Spin, Twist, Nightmare, Exterminator, and myself. Capone will make sure we have plenty of weapons or ammo—whatever we need. He's also clearing out the barn at the pig farm to dispose of any leftovers."

I take another drink of coffee, grunting a bit after it scalds my throat again. "Smiles and the other guys will hang around here. All our family members who're close by will stay here with them, just in case the Twisted Snakes are up to something we aren't aware of. We'll call lockdown and the families will comply. They've been schooled in situations like this, so they won't give us any hassles. Avery, on the other hand, may try to get involved and poke her little nose where it doesn't belong. We can't have that. We want to be ready on any front. These bastards are slimy and already hanging around town. After Avery's shooting, it seems they don't care if we're in a public place or not."

"Yes, I agree with you."

"I need to make it known before I go any further into the details—the fucker who shot Avery is mine. I get to make him suffer for hurting her. It's the least I can do, after her dealing with that shit while with me. The brothers have all acknowledged their acceptance on this, and I need you to do the same." I regard him and wait for him to weigh in on everything I've just told him.

I need to make it crystal fucking clear to everyone— Joker's ass is mine. I'm planning on making that motherfucker wish he was never born, from hurting Avery for no goddamn reason. They have no respect for family members and going after a President's son clearly shows their lack of rules and discipline.

We bikers live by a code. At least most of us do. You don't fuck with people's families. It's a no-go zone for most of the different clubs I've come across over the years.

"If you handle him, then I'll accept this also. I told Avery I will give you a chance, and I mean it, I will." He props his elbows on the bar and rubs the back of his neck.

"All right, cool."

I go into details about what Prez wants us to do and what part each of us will play. Niko is mostly there to be muscle. We'll have a lot of bodies to move—and quickly. We need the big guys and the mean fuckers for this mission.

Those Twisted Snakes won't know what the hell hit them before it's too late.

Ares walks in as I'm finishing up telling Nikoli the plan. He pours himself a cup of coffee and stands on the other side of the bar, directly in front of us.

"Mornin'," he grumbles.

"'Sup, brother," I greet and take a sip of my now normal temperature coffee.

"Good morning, Ares," Nikoli replies with one of his usual formal responses. Fucker doesn't call him princess like he did me.

I'm guessing when he learned English he didn't get the condensed version. Everything's drawn out and sounds elegant. We have an accent being in Texas; we shorten and cut up words, and basically have our own biker lingo. I'm surprised he even understands half the shit we say.

Ares sets his cup down and stands up straight. "You fill him in on the plan?" he mutters and glances my way, picking up that we're talking business.

"Yep, sure did. We just finished discussing it when you walked in." I lean back on my barstool and pop all my knuckles. I hate mornings; my body's always so damn taut.

Nikoli's chair makes a loud scraping sound as he stands. He pushes his chair back in and I smirk. He even has good manners, yet he's a goddamn hitman for the Russian

Mafia. I wonder if he sends his victims family's a sympathy card as well?

No one talks about it, but Prez filled me in on Mr. Good 'ol boy here. He's Tate's bodyguard/best friend and a trained hitman. There's no fooling us with the formal language and suits, we see right through that shit.

Ares and I both watch as he straightens his goofy shirt, "I must go and change if we plan to have mission this evening. I will update Tate and then return in a few hours."

He reaches his right hand out to me. I look down at it; *fuck it.* I reach out and shake his hand.

He smirks and then turns to Ares. "Nice day today, perfect to have your guns out."

Ares cocks his head and looks at Nikoli as if he has lost his mind. "Pardon?" Ares asks gruffly.

"You know, your guns. Like, sun's out, guns out?" he replies and squeezes his bicep.

Ares wears a forlorn expression and I chuckle. "Brother, he's talking about you having your muscles out, like in a beater shirt or sumthin'." I bark a loud laugh, picturing my brother in a shirt that reads, 'suns out guns out'. I should have Avery order him one just to fuck with him about it.

After a beat, it clicks for Ares and he starts to chuckle as well. "Yeah, if I wear my wife beater I'll have all the club cunts around here chasing me all day. Don't want to make the other brothers jealous or nothing," Ares grins good-naturedly and Niko laughs.

"Very good then. Later bikers."

"Later." We both respond in sync and Ares shakes his head at me in a chastising manner as soon as Niko's out the door.

"Don't fucking say it, brother."

"What, man? I haven't said shit."

"It's that look, I know you want to give me shit for that whole wife beater convo' we just had."

"Nah, man, I'm straight. I know Niko says some off-the-wall shit like that sometimes. It's all good."

His brows go up pleased I'm dropping it. "Cool. How's baby girl today?"

"She was still asleep when I left to come fill him in on all the shit happening."

"All right, good. I don't want her upset. We need to take her further next time. She'll enjoy it, with how much fun she had last night."

Taking the last swig of my coffee, I set the cup in front of Ares. He grabs it and places it in the sink for me.

Snickering, I stand and shrug, "Besides, we don't have to worry anyhow. You can just pull your guns out and parade them shits around the club. Ha." I burst into a fit of laughter and Ares glares at me. "Later, bro, I'm about to go check on Shorty."

"Shut the fuck up about that conversation," he grumbles and smirks. "I'll catch up with you later."

"Cool." I continue to laugh to myself and make my way back to my room.

I know that fucker is flipping me off as I walk away. I can feel it boring into my back, begging me to turn around. It's okay though; I'll let him have that one because I have some good shit to give him a hard time about now.

Opening the bedroom door, my gaze shoots straight to the bed, but it's empty. A bunch of rumpled black sheets and my grey comforter hanging off the bed from Avery's wild sleeping habits are left in tow. Checking over the room I notice the bathroom door's closed.

Hmm, she must be in the shower. Fuck yeah.

I'm not going to let this opportunity go to waste, so I strip my clothes off, piece after piece as I make my way to the bathroom. I toss the bundle into the laundry hamper and reach for the door handle. I want to see her before she notices me.

Opening the door quietly so it doesn't make any noise, I peek my head through the opening. I can't see her from this position because of the shower door, so I scoot inside and close the door. Creeping through the tiny bathroom, I'm able to eventually make out Avery's lightly tanned back through the foggy shower door.

She's like a goddess, water trickling over her body in a fluid motion. Her wet hair cascades down her back, outlining the contour of her small curves. Her legs are slightly spread giving me the ultimate view of her firm, round ass.

Reaching down, my palm encloses around my cock, giving it a forceful tug. The length grows and hardens the more I ravish her with my eyes. I could come just watching her like this.

Opening the door, it makes a loud creaky noise and her back stiffens at the unexpected intrusion.

"Relax, Shorty."

Climbing in behind her, I push her hair over her delicate shoulder so I can sample the sweet skin on her neck. Running my hand over one of her exposed peaks, I tweak it and her lips part in response. Her little breaths key me in on what she enjoys, and, in turn, drives me on to explore and learn more about her body. I skim my fingers down her silky skin until I reach her plump lips, leading me to her wet core.

"2." It leaves her in a quiet moan.

I wouldn't have heard it with the noise from the water, but having her body so close to mine, I make out the weak plea. She wants this as much as I do. She's always ready for me.

"I'm here," I whisper next to her ear.

She slowly turns in my arms and her warm honey irises are scorching with lust when she sees my body. Little water droplets run over her lips and they entice me to take a sample. Bending, I press a soft kiss her top lip then repeat with a kiss to her bottom lip.

Her mouth opens again and I taste her sweet breath as she exhales. *Strawberries*, she tastes like a red, ripe, juicy strawberry.

I savor it as I take her lips with mine, this time it's not chaste, it's full of want and need. My tongue caresses hers as I take my time exploring her succulent mouth. Her palms press slightly against my chest and I hold her tight to me.

I'm not finished yet. I take her mouth more forcefully, and I feel her surrender in my arms. She gives in and kisses me back with just as much fervor. She grips my shoulders firmly, flexing her fingers as the kiss deepens and she holds her weight off her injured leg

She pulls away, gasping, attempting to replenish the air in her lungs. Her lips carry a cherry shade from our kiss. The sight of her like this has me groaning. She's ravishing.

I want to take her so hard right now. I have an internal need to claim her, mark her as mine in this moment. Avery, on the other hand, has different ideas.

She leans in and bites my pec savagely. "Ah, fuck, free bird." I yelp, not too manly either and grasp her hair tightly in my fist.

She sucks the skin around the sore area and leisurely makes her way down my toned stomach to my engorged cock. I fist her hair with one hand and grip her bicep in the other. She needs to be careful she doesn't rip those stitches and hurt herself.

My head falls back, my eyes fining the ceiling as she takes me deeply in her mouth, going as far she can. *Christ that feels phenomenal.* She swirls her tongue around the ridge of my dick and I blink several times to concentrate on not jerking her closer and forcing myself further into her throat.

Clearing my suddenly choked up throat, I watch her head bob up and down my dick for a few minutes. "Enough, Avery," I groan, thoroughly aroused, and she looks up at me from below. Her mouth is wrapped tightly around my cock and her eyes are wide. She looks so fucking innocent and beautiful like this.

Holding her bicep, I carefully pull her back up in front of me. "You're too good at that, Shorty. You almost made me lose control," I admit and nod toward the shower wall.

She grins at me, her velvety voice letting loose a pleased chuckle. She turns her head slightly and I spin her by her hip so she faces the wall again. I keep hold of her hip as I press down on her back, moving her closer to the wall.

"Brace yourself, baby, I don't want to hurt you."

"Okay, 2. Like this?" She widens her arms and attempts to get a good grip on the soap fixtures attached to the tiles.

"Yeah, perfect." Spreading her legs apart, easily with my knees, I line my cock up to her sopping wet entrance. I push in slightly, not putting too much weight on her.

"Oh yes," she moans and I thrust in deeper.

I wrap my hand around her waist, placing my palm firmly over her clit. Spreading my fingers on each side of her entrance so I can feel myself each time I move in and pull out of her. Her tight cunt drips each time I pull myself out to the tip and each time, I lose my breath. She's beyond perfect.

"Fuck, Avery, you feel so good like this, tight and wet. Squeeze that pussy, baby," I order as she grips my cock snugly.

"Ha-harder, please."

"I'm gonna' hurt your leg, baby."

"No 2, I need it harder."

Gripping her hip with my other hand, I apply pressure to her clit simultaneously with my other palm and hammer into her.

"Yes." She whimpers and I flex my fingers, increasing my momentum. I start to slam into her roughly, not being able to control the lust consuming my body.

She lays her head against the shower wall and takes each thrust I give her.

"Fuck, Shorty, I'm about to come." Bending over, I sink my teeth into her back.

It sets her off and I feel her hot center grip me repeatedly as she calls out. My dick tingles in an intense explosion of pleasure and my thick cum spurts into her. As I come, I pull her back to my chest, holding her in an iron grip as I empty myself. We stand like that, panting, attempting to catch our breath after the quick, intense time we just shared together.

"Holy shit; I don't know if I can walk after that," she admits, stills breathless, setting a chuckle free from me.

I squeeze her to me and kiss her cheek sweetly. "It's all good. After that, I'll carry you if you want. Hell, I should be carrying you around anyhow to keep the weight off your thigh." She giggles and it's a beautiful sound to hear. "It seems to keep getting better, yeah?" I mumble as her irises meet mine.

Her eyes grow tender as she peers up at me, "Yeah, it's always been good, but it's turned phenomenal. I know this is all fun and stuff but—"

"No," I interrupt her before she can finish. "Don't go there. Just roll with whatever we're doing and feeling. I know you like being free and so do I, but we don't have to analyze this shit right the fuck now, okay?"

"Uh, yeah, I won't scrutinize stuff right now," she agrees.

I press another kiss to her cheek and grab the towel hanging from the side of the shower to dry her off.

"Good girl." I wrap the towel around her frame to keep her warm, not leaving a drop behind. "I need to go over some shit about tonight with you."

She appears a little surprised and intrigued, "Tonight? What's going on?"

"Me and some of the guys are going out on business. I need you to stay here and inside the building. London and Jamison will be here too so you guys can chill."

She scrunches her forehead and opens her mouth. I already expected she'd argue or attempt to butt in.

"Is everything okay?" I watch as she pulls her clothes on.

"Everything's straight. Don't worry your pretty head, baby."

"Can I do something to help?"

"Nope, just stay here and out of trouble."

"I'm never in trouble," she grumbles, disgruntled.

I put on a fresh pair of boxer briefs and socks. The rest of my clothes can be jacked up, but underwear and socks always have to be clean. "Ah, yeah, you're definitely trouble, especially when you get around London."

"Well, maybe, but London's calmed down a lot since she had the baby. Plus, I'm not going to act crazy or anything in your club when you're not going to be here. It'll be weird though, being here without you."

"It'll be fine; you take it easy and enjoy yourself." I put on black jeans, a black T-shirt, and boots.

"I wish you'd just tell me what's going on. You look like you're going to go rob a place dressed in all black." She grins and points to my attire.

"Already pulling the wifey card and you ain't even my ol' lady yet, huh?" I chuckle and she beams.

"No, I can sense when someone's up to something."

"Oh, now you have super powers too?"

"No, stop teasing me," she giggles and I pull her in for a hug.

"When're you leaving?"

Damn it, I thought I had her distracted.

"Probably in a couple hours, Nikoli wanted to change then rest up and shit."

"Niko's going with you?" she asks as I walk and she sort of hobbles to the dining room.

"Yeah, he's going to chill with us for a minute."

We reach the dining area and there's a giant six-foot-long sub sandwich laid out with paper plates next to it. "Looks like this is lunch today, you want some?"

"Definitely, that looks yummy."

I load her up a plate with part of the sub and some chips, then load mine up with double the amount. Every time she visits, we take turns taking care of each other. I'll take her to get food or she might cook us something. This time, I'm doing it all with her hurt. I want her taking it easy.

Relinquish

It's domestic and we tend to lean the other way on that aspect, but it's still nice. I enjoy doing things for her and making her happy. She seems to feel the same way about it too.

Avery

I don't know what the hell's going on around here, but something's obviously up. These guys are prowling around like they're going on a top-secret mission. I wish I could find out what it was. It's not like I can snoop around or anything. There're members or family in every room.

As soon as Niko gets here, I'm going to ask. I can usually break through his wall and get him to let me know stuff he wouldn't normally tell anyone else. I've become sort of his American sister. I don't say that out loud, though, considering what happened to his real sisters in Russia. I can't think of that stuff right now though. I have to keep trying to eavesdrop.

I find London planted on the sofa holding Jamison while he naps and join her. Kid ran around like crazy and as

173

soon as he sat on her lap to relax, he conked out. Like literally ten seconds and he was fast asleep with his little mouth hanging open. London swears Cain sleeps the same way, but if Cain's not naked then I don't really care. I've told her that in the past, and she thinks it's hilarious.

Little guy pretty much runs the club when he's here too. Every member pays attention and plays around with him. It's adorable seeing a bunch of big, burly bikers chasing around a miniature Cain and feeding him a grip of junk food. I bet Jamison loves coming here. I wouldn't be surprised if that kid heads up the club one day.

"Hey, chickadee." She beams a, bright smile.

"Hi, lady," I sit next to her.

My leg still hurts badly so I've been sitting a lot and trying not to walk around much. I know I'm a weenie, but I'm not admitting to anyone that it hurts. "So, it's driving me crazy, but do you know what's really going on?" I try my hand at gossiping. London's like Fort Knox, though. These Oath Keepers have no clue just how loyal she is to them.

"No, Cain told me we needed to be here and stay inside. I trust him though. I know he's protecting us."

"Yeah, it just drives me crazy that 2 won't tell me. I mean, I'm new to this so some details would be nice."

"Well, if you really like 2 Piece then get used to it. That's club business and this is club life. They don't share anything with anyone. Maybe a little more than nothing if you're an ol' lady."

"Ha, yeah right, I won't be anyone's ol' lady or wife anytime soon. So, does that mean Cain tells you more?"

She shrugs. "No, he doesn't, and I don't ask either. I'm telling you, Avery, if you plan to stick around; you have to fight through that need to know everything. You're an inquisitive person, but they're protective men—each one of them. They'll only do what needs to be done."

"How can you be so okay with everything and the not knowing part?"

"I'm fine with it because I love Cain and have accepted his way of life as my own."

"Ugh, I'll try to not be so nosey. It may drive me nuts, but I'll try because I care for 2. I also don't want to be known as a busybody or a nagger. He already joked about me acting like a 'wifey'. I thought I'd pass out with that word, but surprisingly it didn't affect me like I thought it would."

"I'm surprised; you know 2 Piece doesn't usually hang with the same chick like he's done with you." Jamison stirs in her arms and she rocks him slightly. He goes back to his cute baby snores after a few minutes.

"Well, we haven't hung together or anything. I mean, just when I visit," I admit quietly.

"That's what I'm talking about. He doesn't see chicks over and over. Just you, so that means you're special to him."

"I don't know about all of that," I scoff, waving her off.

"It's true. You may not see it, but we do," she acknowledges, and I smile.

Does he really feel strongly for me? I hope so, but I'm scared he doesn't. I don't want to be that attached anyhow. I love my freedom. I wonder how it'd be, since he's different than the other guys I've dated. I wonder if he'd stay thoughtful and spontaneous or even be faithful. Who knows?

We watch TV for about thirty minutes then Cain and 2 Piece come walking over with serious expressions. 2 might be dressed like he's going to rob someone, but he still looks completely smoking hot. His chest and arms are well defined in his plain T-shirt and his black jeans hug his ass nicely. His tattoos snake out from all directions and it's a pleasant reminder of what I got to see in the shower earlier today.

Cain bends down to talk softly to London and embraces her lovingly.

"Hey, Shorty, you good?" He pulls me up from the couch, helping me stand in front of him.

I give him a small smirk and nod. "Yes, I'm fine. Are you okay? Is everything all right? You look so serious."

"Everything's straight, Avery. I told you, don't worry. You're so curious all the damn time."

"I know and I don't mean to be, it's just my nature. I can't help it if I want everything to be kosher and you to be happy."

"I know, free bird, don't sweat it. I'll be back soon, you be a good girl, yeah?"

"I will."

"Promise me."

"I do."

"Good," he mutters against my lips, and I melt a little inside.

This man is so delectable; I just want to eat him up. He places his hands on each side of my face and lavishes kisses on me. The guys all start teasing in the background, but I ignore it. It's in this kiss that I feel it for the first time.

It's as if he's pouring his whole heart into this kiss and it's a truly serene feeling. I run my hands under his shirt over his firm muscles, until I rest them on his chest and kiss him back with the same passion. If he's going to show me his soul, then I'll show him pieces of mine in return. I'm falling and I don't know if it's a good or a bad thing.

Eventually he pulls back pausing with his face close to mine, our noses touch and we exchange breaths. He lazily opens his eyes, peering straight into mine with wonder. There's so much we need to say, but hold back.

Our spell's broken when Ares calls to him. "Hey, 2, time to roll out, brother. Pack it into Loretta."

"Cool," 2 Piece replies and turns back to me. There're unspoken words screaming at me from his eyes, and I know this isn't over. Hopefully it's merely the beginning, if that kiss is any indication.

Licking my lips, I give a nod, never breaking eye contact.

He blinks and I see it register that I'm on the same page as he is. "I'll see you soon, free bird." He gives me a chaste kiss then turns and walks toward Ares and the other brothers.

That was surreal. I'm still processing everything that just happened in that brief kiss we shared.

And why the hell are they taking Cain's car, Loretta? They're bikers. What do they need with a car?

2 Piece

"You already got everything loaded up?" I ask Ares and Cain as I sit in the back seat.

Loretta rumbles loudly as Cain starts her up and gives her gas. Car is a fuckin' beast. I don't even think you can classify this thing as a car anymore. It's just awesome.

Ares's riding in the passenger side and Cain's driving. Twist and I are sitting in the back and the other guys are following us in the van.

"Yeah, brother, we have all the stuff ready. We just have to get close enough to their club to execute the plan,"

Ares hollers over Cain's music. Cain's blasting Korn through his badass sound system.

"If we're worried about getting close, why in the fuck are we bringing Loretta? This bitch is loud as fuck. You can hear her from down the street and that's not even when Cain stomps on it."

"The other van took a shit earlier," Twist supplies.

"Well that blows. Hope we can fit all those serpent fucks in one van. We should've brought my truck."

Cain calls over his shoulder. "Nah, brother, we can fit like four of them in my trunk if needed; don't worry about it."

Well fuck it, if they've worked it out, I'm going to sit back and relax before shit gets real.

Twist turns to me and sneers. "I can't wait to put the gas in their air vents. Those Snakes won't ever see it coming. Stupid bitches." He snickers and I grin at his excitement.

Truth is, I can't wait until we do it either.

We've got to get close enough to their club so we can run the toxic gas straight through their air duct. None of them will see it coming until it's too late. It'll be when they're all passed out and sitting ducks too, so even more perfect.

"Have any of you tried this before? Prez said he pulled it off with no issues but have y'all actually done it?" I glance at everyone in the car.

It's silent except for the radio blaring. Cain chews on his bottom lip, Twist stares out his window, and Ares taps his fingers in rhythm to the music.

"Fuck, seriously? I hope this shit pops off without any issues. I won't be getting shot on this little outing. I already know from first-hand experience those assholes will shoot first," I grimace, a touch nervous now.

"Relax, 2. Everything will work out accordingly and we'll have us a hog fest, the way we plan to." Ares attempts to reassure me. "I wouldn't let them get to you anyhow." He admits a moment later, much quieter.

Not sure how reassuring that is, I mean, so he believes in the plan. That's good, but that doesn't mean I do. I had way too much shit in life go wrong, for me to suddenly start having faith in random shit. I don't fucking think so. I'm one of those fools with not only a Plan A or Plan B, but I have a Plan C in the works as well. Tonight, though, if this goes south, my ass is straight up shooting these clowns.

We drive for about two hours before we pull up close to their clubhouse. They're not as secluded as our club, but there are still plenty of trees for us to hide behind. Cain parks his Challenger behind a cluster of bushes so it won't be seen easily.

We climb out as the van pulls in behind us. Cain pops the trunk and it's half full of random supplies. I check my weapons to make sure they're loaded and ready to go. Ares hands me a backpack to carry, full of blindfolds and zip ties.

I put it on and pace restlessly.

"Okay, I'm ready," Spin declares and pulls his hoodie over his head.

He's good at putting machines and various things together, so he's going to be the one to hook everything up. We creep to the side of a building next to the club. It appears as if it might be an old abandoned garage. Surprisingly there's no one around outside, but it sounds like they have a huge party going on inside.

We watch as Nightmare cuts through the metal fence, bends it back and follows Spin through the gaping hole. No missing that cut job, it's like five feet tall and two feet wide. The only thing we seem to be lacking is a large yellow flag to put next to it. My heart is beating so fast, watching them creep through the Snakes' compound yard.

Shit, I hope there aren't any dogs or anything.

A sudden "Hey," gets yelled out and then there's silence again, besides the music pounding through their walls. This is ideal. Spin has to drill a small portion on the roof to get to the AC. All the noise from the music will provide adequate cover for the guys to do their job.

"Crazy fuckers, I hope this works," Cain whispers and Ares shoots him an irritated glance.

Ares' phone vibrates after a few minutes and he checks the message. A look of relief sweeps his features and he glances at us. "Hole's drilled in the roof, they were in the wrong spot so they had to drill a second hole. They got to the

181

AC air duct line and are about to attach the tube inside it and turn on the gas. Spin said to watch for anyone coming outside feeling' funny and shit."

I stare at the building, waiting for anything at all to happen. Twist lets out a joyous snicker, excited. It sounds creepy as fuck. I'm counting my blessings I'm not his enemy.

"Night is going to text when the gas tanks are completely empty. We'll meet them in front and out back of the club. Just like we'd discussed, we'll split up into teams. We bust in the doors and collect our dues."

I breathe deeply. Shit's about to get real. There's a crunching sound behind us and we all turn as one to investigate. I have my hand on one of my pieces ready just in case.

"What? I get nervous and have to piss," Cain says with his hands up in a position of surrender. Then he whips his cock out and starts pissing out in the open.

Twist plucks at his shirt and you can see his chest heave with deep breaths. Guess I'm not the only one feeling antsy.

"Hurry up for fuck's sake," Ares growls, and I grin at Cain.

He returns it and flips me off. *Dumb ass.* It'd be funny to see Ares drop kick the shit out of him though.

Ares' phone vibrates again and he quickly checks it. "All right, brothers, it's time. Cain, put your cock away. Twist, calm the fuck down, and 2, quit your goddamn pacing. You fucks are getting me wound up and we have to be focused to execute this perfectly."

"I'm calm," Twist mumbles. Cain gets back to the group and gives Ares a big smile just to fuck with him.

"You all go to the front. I'm meeting Spin and Nightmare out back. We'll meet you guys in the middle. Exterminator, back the van up as close as possible to the front door."

"Yep." Ex nods and heads for the van.

Ares turns to us, serious now. "If the gas doesn't work, kill them all."

I nod and pull both of my Glocks out to be ready. Twist unsnaps his blade holder so he can easily whip his knife out if needed; Cain grabs his Glock as well. Cain heads for the front door with us following quietly. Ex passes us in the van driving slowly with the lights off.

The Snakes should be fucked up from all the toxic fumes, but it's best to still be careful just in case. As we make our way to the front door the only sounds are from the music inside, no voices of any kind. I check in one of the windows, but can't see anything. It's probably covered with black paint. I feel like we're about to walk into a den full of vampires or some crazy shit like that.

"Bro, I feel like we're on the set of a horror movie," Cain whispers, reading my mind.

"No shit, man, it's creepy. Just remember these fuckers will shoot you; it ain't a fucking movie."

"You pussies, man up," Twist sneers, and I scowl at him.

"You call me pussy like it's a bad thing. I fuck 'em, eat 'em, and enjoy looking at 'em. Ain't a fucking thing wrong with pussy, brother," I snarl back at him, and Cain steps between us.

"Seriously, you guys are going to do this shit now? Save it for later. Y'all are going to get us killed."

I roll my eyes, brushing it off and head for the door. I'm sick of fucking around already. I have no patience for Twist's moody ass.

The front door flies open and we jump back about a foot. We each have our Glocks pointed in front of us, ready to shoot whoever poses a threat. Nightmare pokes his head out and grins menacingly at us. Dude's scary as fuck with his long dark hair and dark eyes.

Cain grabs his chest dramatically. "Fuckin' A, brother, you about gave me a goddamn heart attack and shit!" he inhales a few deep breaths.

Exterminator walks past us with an eyebrow raised. He's probably bored with Nightmare by now since they're always around each other.

Twist swaggers past us and shoulder checks me. "Come on, bitches," he says snarkily.

That's it. I'm so tired of this little motherfucker and his mouth. He may be crazy, but I'm no fucking punk. I smash back into him and shoulder check him hard enough he bumps into the doorway.

"The fuck?" he yells and slams his hands against my chest.

Motherfucker wants to do this, we'll fucking do it. I'm already on edge looking forward to fucking up this Joker character.

Cain jumps in front of me quickly. "Calm down, brother. Not here, it's the wrong time to do this. Chill, man," he holds my shoulders.

No getting past this asshole; he's strong as fuck always training to fight. "I'm sick of his motherfucking comments. He wants to see a bitch; I'll make him my fucking bitch." I promise.

Twist sticks his tongue out and licks up his arm sickly. "Bitch, huh? You've never done any fucking time. What do you know about making a bitch? I can teach you, I'll train you just like I did my last bitch. *Bitch...*" Twist cackles and it's like nails on a chalkboard to my ears.

Nightmare snatches Twist around the arm and drags him into the clubhouse before I can say anything. The stupid fucker; I'll get his ass later. I thought Capone was a fucking pansy ass, but clearly it's Twist.

Cain shakes his head sternly. "Dude, calm down, Twist will go fucking manic."

"I don't give a shit if you're all buddies with his ass because of London. I won't let him disrespect me."

"I know, 2, trust. I don't blame you, not here though. We're on a mission and could get ourselves killed because you two are acting like dipshits."

I nod. *Yeah, yeah, I get it.* This isn't over though.

"How about you go sit in the van and drive that. We'll get these dicks loaded, and then you can take some anger out on them at the ranch. Ex was supposed to stay out here, but he took it upon himself to go inside instead," Cain suggests rationally.

"All right, guess I'll cool off and get my head on straight." I agree, not wanting to get anyone killed by me being stubborn. I'll save it for the bastard Snakes.

It's times like this; I wouldn't mind having a smoke.

Avery

I wonder what they're doing and why I couldn't go with them. They're up to something and Niko's ass never showed up either. I hope 2's okay and safe.

"Hey, girl, would you be a doll and get me a Dr. Pepper from the bar?" London asks sweetly.

"Yeah, of course. Can I go back there or do I ask one of the guys?"

"No, you can go back there and get whatever you want. If there's a bartender then ask, otherwise help yourself."

I nod and go behind the bar. I'm filling up London's soda and my Sprite, when Capone comes sauntering over.

"Hey, suga'. Whatcha' doing?"

"Hi. I'm not your 'sugar', I'm Avery and I'm seeing 2 Piece. As for what I'm doing-I'm getting London a drink. Would you like me to get you something while I'm back here?" I try to be polite, but I'm not some saucy ass he can call pet names.

He scrunches his nose, "I thought you were club ass. I heard Ares talking to 2 Piece about you. So, you'll fuck them both, but not me?"

"Seriously? You really just asked if I would fuck you? No way, I won't sleep with random men. And to set the record straight, I did not fuck Ares." I'm flustered and that irritates me even more, letting this ass get me wound up.

"You couldn't handle my shit anyhow. 2 Piece likes to fuck a lot, so don't get too comfortable," he utters rudely as Prez walks up behind him.

He shoots Capone an irritated look. "'Pone, go chill with Smiles and leave 2's bitch alone," he barks out, and Capone walks off without a word. "Sorry about that, doll. He's a little jealous of 2, I think."

187

I give him a friendly smile. "It's okay. Would you like me to get you something?"

"Yep, that'd be good. How about a Corona and some water." He takes a seat at the bar and I go to work finding what he wants. "Nice having a makeshift bartender here. Usually I have to see one of these guy's ugly mugs serving me." He smirks.

"Well enjoy your drink; I have to drop this off with London. Poor thing's stuck under a heavy, sleeping baby."

He nods. "Real fast, ignore Capone, he's an ass. I wanted to let you know that I'm glad you came for a visit. 2's been lonely a lot, he's had a rough life growing up. Most probably don't see it, but I notice more shit. Anyhow, he's happy around you." He finishes and takes a pull from the beer.

I beam at his words, "Thank you, that means a lot." He returns my smile and I take the drinks to go sit back by London. She was watching the whole thing and it doesn't surprise me when she instantly starts peppering questions.

"So, what was that about? Why did Capone look pissed and why were you smiling at Prez all goofy."

I recount what happened and she shakes her head, rolling her eyes. "Capone's a douche. I'm surprised Cain hasn't throttled his ass yet. Listen to Prez, he's a smart guy."

"Yeah, that's what I figured. I'm just glad that someone notices I make 2 happy. He makes me very happy. I'm scared how I'm starting to feel for him, you know?"

"I get it girl; Cain swept me straight off my feet," she murmurs wistfully.

"It's hitting me now. I think about him nonstop when I'm not around to be honest. I feel like he's becoming more of an obsession each time I visit. I don't want to get my heart broken though. I guess the only reason I'm not too scared to get serious with him, is I know he likes his freedom as much as I do. We both love to just take off and not be tied down or anything. Not to mention, he's also a little wild which fits me perfectly. We all know I love to party when I'm in the mood."

She starts nodding and laughing. "Yes, I specifically remember the first night I met you. We got bum-ass drunk and you puked the next morning," she recounts through her giggles.

I laugh loudly thinking about us all waking up naked and Emily freaking out. "That was such a blast. But God, I thought I was going to die."

"Ugh, me too. Emily definitely needed some fun before dealing with all that craziness with her ex." I get quiet and look away. "You know he'll be fine. The guys will make sure he's safe."

"I know, but I can't shake this feeling I have for some reason, and then we bring up that situation with Emily." I hold my stomach and swallow a few times, trying to make it go away. I glance around the room at everyone and watch Capone as he steps out of the club and the door slams closed.

Good, I at least won't have to deal with him for a while.

189

2 Piece

I squint at the oncoming headlights and attempt to make out the vehicle approaching. It looks like a truck. I think it's probably Niko since he was running a little behind us.

The guys are busy zip tying and blindfolding the Twisted Snakes we just gassed. I can't wait until we get to the ranch and I can teach that fucker a lesson for shooting Avery.

"Expecting company?" Exterminator questions as he shoulders off one of the Snakes into the back of the van.

"Yeah, that blue truck is Nikoli, the Russian we were waiting on,"

"Ah, got it." he walks off toward the clubhouse again.

Nikoli parks his truck and climbs out, shutting the door quietly. "Are they ready?" he checks his gun.

"Yep, sure are. They're loading the bodies now."

He nods and heads to the entrance. I'm glad to see he decided to change into something more fit for this outing. There'll more than likely be a lot of blood, so we all need to wear black.

"Oof." I turn and see Cain stretching out his back.

"'Sup, brother?" I cock my head.

"That's a fat fucker; he about killed my back."

I chuckle and he takes off for another. Ten minutes later and the brothers have the bodies loaded up. We didn't need Cain's trunk after all. They threw a couple in the back of Niko's truck and covered them with a tarp, it worked perfectly. We should've done that with the others as well.

Exterminator climbs into the passenger seat next to me and Nightmare gets in the back of the van with the passed-out scumbags.

"Let's move, 2, before any dumb asses show up being nosey." Ex grumbles.

"All right, cool."

Starting the van, we begin the journey to the ranch. The miles pass slowly; as I concentrate on watching the speed limit. I'd normally fly down Texas highways, but I have to be cautious with the bodies in the back. The Eagles play low as we each seem to be in our own little world.

I wonder when we'll be done so I can get back to Avery. I hope she's doing okay. I'm sure she is; she has London with her.

I'm glad my shorty seems to be recovering more from the shot. Her stiches are healing up nicely the last time I checked and she hasn't complained much about it. Who knew that girl would be such a trooper.

We've been riding for about an hour when I hear some moaning and rustling. That can't be Nightmare; was he shot or something? Surely Ex would've said something if Night was injured.

"You all right back there, Nightmare?" I peer into the rearview mirror.

"Turn on the back light," he gripes.

Flicking on the light, Exterminator turns so he can see in the back. I hear a thud and a grunt. The van rocks with the heavy movement. *What the hell?*

"Fuck!" Ex yells out and turns to me. I glance back and see Nightmare's arm dripping blood and he has someone pinned down. "We have one awake already. You need to find a place to pull the fuck over."

"Yeah, bro, I'll take the closest exit. I think it's three miles up."

Ex turns back around to keep an eye on Nightmare and the others. "You straight, Night?" he removes his own blade.

"He fucking sliced me, why wasn't he secured? Hurry up," he snarls angrily.

"I am, brother, just a sec," I call towards the back, loudly, so he can hear me. There's some more rustling and then pissed off murmuring.

I hate having to make an unscheduled stop. You never know what could happen. Cops are always hiding where you least need them to be, and what if there are more Snakes not secured properly? I've never done any time and I'd like to not start now — for kidnapping and whatever else they can find to cook up.

I take the exit to a little rest area. It's surrounded by plenty of trees so I drive around toward the back of the building. There are some worn-out covered picnic tables and a few large trash dumpsters.

"All right, Ex, you go around and I'll stay here with my weapon trained on them until you get asshat unloaded."

He nods and jumps out of the dark van. The back door flies open a moment later. Night holds the scum down and Ex stabs the guy in the ribs then in the opposite leg. "

Ain't going to get far now, buttercup," Exterminator chuckles, and Nightmare rolls the Snake out the back of the van by kicking him repeatedly.

Niko and Cain pull up behind the vehicle with the rest of the guys. They approach the van carefully.

"It's all good, brothers. We had one wake up and Night got sliced, so we're dealing with him now."

Twist gets a pleasantly surprised look on his face. Ex has his gun trained on the tied-up idiots so I make my way to where they are surrounding the douche that woke. "So, what are we going to do with this one?" I mutter curiously.

Nightmare turns to me; he might as well be the grim reaper right now with that look gracing his features. The scar running from eyebrow to his nose, makes him seem even more dangerous.

"I'll take care of the problem," he grits then pulls out his gun and shoots the guy in both his legs.

"Ah!" The guy screams in pain and the brothers snicker. I remain silent, watching, and taking note of the Nomads' methods.

Nightmare snatches the screaming man by his wrists and drags him toward the dumpster. "Anybody got some gas?" he glances at each of us.

"Of course," Nikoli responds and grabs a gas can out of his truck bed.

Night nods at Ex. Exterminator grasps the man's legs as Night holds his wrists and they fling him into the dumpster. "Now the fun part," he mutters cryptically. He pours gas over the opening of the dumpster; the man wails inside and I scan the surroundings to make sure no one is near.

Nightmare pulls out his plain zippo and lights a piece of trash, then throws it into the dumpster. The bin erupts into a blueish gold blaze, burning the gas away. The Twisted Snake wails bone-chilling screams, and I try to hold my breath. The smell of burning flesh is ripe and makes me gag. Twist watches me and grins evilly.

That's my cue to make my way back to the van and most of the guys follow suit.

If Avery only knew how much of a bad man I was. I don't deserve someone as kind and good as her. Fuck, it's going to be hard to sleep tonight next to her, after this.

Exterminator and Nightmare load up in the van and it's so silent I could hear crickets. I look back at Night in the mirror. He has his shirt off and wrapped around his arm. The cut's not deep, just long, so it's making a mess.

"Now you know why we're Nomads, brother. We tend to not fit in so much with everyone else," Ex explains and stares solemnly out the front window.

"Yep, now I know. Although I want to do something similar to the dirt bag that shot Avery," I admit, and he looks at me skeptically for a few beats. I don't cower and he nods in acceptance.

"We can make it happen then, brother," he admits, and I drive toward the ranch again. That was just one brief hiccup in what's to come tonight, I'm sure.

Avery

I tried calling 2 Piece but never got any response. London thinks I'm being paranoid and tells me to leave the guys alone to do what they need to do. I don't get how she can be so calm. She clearly has more faith in Cain doing his job.

I on the other hand have no idea what 2's job is. I know he does the *long runs*, whatever that means. This is the first time I've been around him and he's let me know something's up. That means we're making progress if he's opening up to me about things he normally keeps quiet.

I'm bored, so I may as well call my parents.

"Hello." My dad's voice brings a feeling of warmth and comfort to me. I miss my dad a lot. I think if my mom wasn't around so much, then I'd visit him more.

"Hey, Dad."

"Oh, honeybee! So nice to hear from you. How ya' been, kid?"

"I'm doing really good, Dad, how about you?"

"Oh, same ol' same ol', you know; this old man doesn't do much. I went and watched the dolphins this morning with your mom, and then she went to work."

"That's awesome, I miss working with the animals and watching the dolphins."

"All the more reason for you to come on home."

"Dad, you've been trying for a while now and it hasn't worked."

"You can't blame me for trying to get my only daughter back close to me."

"Maybe, I'll see if my friend wants to take a ride out there sometime soon."

"That's great, hon. Is this Miss Emily?"

"No, it's a guy I've been seeing for a while."

"A guy? But you've never really introduced us to guys before."

"I know, Dad; that's how you know this one's kind of special."

"Well, if he's won my girl over, then I'm certainly intrigued to meet him."

"I'll discuss it with him and give you a call when we know more, okay?"

"All right, stay safe. I love you."

"I love you, too, Dad. Tell Mom hi for me."

"I will, bye, kiddo."

"Bye."

I can't believe I told him we might visit. Where on earth did that idea come from? I'm surprised he didn't get all bossy about it, but that's more my mom, not him. I need to talk to 2 about the feelings I'm developing.

2 Piece

We drive down the long, dark, dirt road that leads to the ranch. It's going to be a busy night ahead; I'm looking forward to this much-deserved retribution. Our friends and families shouldn't have to live in fear of being hurt and terrorized by another club.

The trip's been silent and I'm jonesin' to get the fuck out of this van. I pull up to the side of the giant, faded white barn. There won't be anyone coming this way, but better safe than sorry.

Jumping out in a hurry, I'm grateful to stretch my legs and be out of the tight space. Ex steps in front of me before I make it to the back door of the vehicle to let Night out, "Whose bikes are parked out front?" he murmurs quietly.

"One is Capone's. He's supposed to make sure the barns all ready for us. I don't know who the other's is."

"You checking that shit out?"

I raise my eyebrow. He's serious right now? I just told him it's Capone. He looks at me solemnly. *Fuck it. Guess I'm going in.*

"Sure, I'll go check on Capone, if it will keep your panties out of a wad," I grumble, exasperated, and he shakes his head, blowing me off to open the door for Nightmare.

The building illuminates more with the oncoming headlights of Niko's truck and the night rumbles with the sound of Cain's Challenger following the truck. It all feeds into the headache I'm starting to get. Tonight's just not my night.

I'm grumpy and would rather be spending time with Avery. I know she'll be leaving to go back sometime soon now that we are taking care of this shit. I wonder how she'd feel if I was to drive her up after Nikoli left. I'll have to discuss it with her.

Maybe I'll see if Ares wants to go, too. We could have some fun with her before we leave Tennessee to come back home. I don't want to think of coming back without her and he might make the trip more bearable.

Opening the weathered barn door, it creaks loudly as I slip through. The smell of hay and dust hits me and I place my shirt over my nose until I get used to it. It's so dark inside. The old dingy light globe at the very top of the barn is useless, and I can't see more than five steps in front of me.

It's just enough to give everything an eerie shadow and make your eyes play tricks. I squint, trying to make out specific shapes. "Capone?" I call into the silent barn and it echoes slightly.

The brothers talking and making noises seep through the weathered cracks and I make out a few different conversations between them.

I feel it against my back—the cold stiffness—before I hear the click that seems to echo throughout the entire barn. I put my hands out to each side of my head, palms flat, pointing forward, then stand stock still and slow my breathing. I don't know who the fuck's behind me or what's going on right now. I'm not going to chance it and try to play the hero though.

The only thing that runs through my head, is that one of the Snakes must've found out our plan. It pains me to believe we have a rat in our club, but it seems as if it's the only feasible answer. "Look, there are about twenty other bikers outside this barn. You really don't want to be doing this right now."

"Fucking lyin' bitch. There's only seven outside." I hear his voice and chills spread over my body. I can't fucking believe this is happening right now. Is he crazy? Is he completely ignorant of what he is doing to himself right now?

"Capone, man, what the fuck's going on?"

"It's simple; you're each going to die," he chortles cockily. "Hey, Joker, this is the one you wanted. He came right to us."

As soon as I hear the name Joker my body goes rigid, on high alert. Fuck, he wasn't at the club with the rest of them. This is what we were worried about, them not all being there.

What am I going do? I can't let my brothers get hurt. I refuse to carry that on my shoulders if I make it out of here okay.

Joker swaggers over to me with his top lip curled in a snarl. I remember that ghostlike figure perfectly. He damn near glows in here compared to the dingy surroundings.

"Well, look who we have. It's the cunt that ran from me on my bike. Fucking coward," he spits angrily, close to my face.

It takes every ounce of self-control I possess not to head butt him as the word coward leaves his mouth. I can only savor the visualization of my forehead meeting his nose with a loud crack and the sickening spray of blood erupting. I know if I do it, the repercussions would be me getting shot and not protecting my club that is right outside that old door.

I swallow my pride and remain quiet. He'll more than likely give me some useful information if I stick with a lackluster expression. I hear the brothers chortle and pray they decide to not come in after me.

"What next, Joker?" Capone probes and digs the gun deeper into my back. *Fuck that hurts.* I'm going to mess up this fucker so badly if I get free from this.

Joker's eyes light up with ideas I'm sure I'm not keen on hearing. "First we need to move him out of the way before the rest come in here. We sneak him out the back where I took off those boards. We'll get him out there, and once the rest of the club comes in, we'll torch this shit hole. Teach these fucks to try to kidnap my club. I'm going to find something to tie him up with."

"No problem," Capone agrees happily as Joker walks behind some equipment.

"Capone, why are you doing this? Why betray your brothers?"

"My brothers? Are you kidding me? You all treat me like shit there. I was just trying to talk to that piece of ass you have at the club and she was a fucking bitch too. No, my *brothers* are the guys you've tied up out there. My real brother just went to get something to secure your ass with."

"Your real brother? Joker's your kin?"

I need to keep him talking while it's only him; I have to figure a way out of this. The only rational thing I can think of is to scream to my brothers that it's a trap. However, I don't know if they'd try to come get me or if these idiots would start randomly shooting and kill one of them.

"Yep, our father used to be President of the Twisted Snakes. Then Brently's stupid ass had to start seeing Seraphina. We don't take kindly to our sister seeing some fuck face kid of another club."

Bingo, all the pieces come together. I can't believe this shit. Capone's been around for about four years.

"Capone, they haven't been seeing each other for four years."

"Oh, I know. I've been stealing guns and club money the whole time I've been with the Oath Keepers. There're a lot of us who get into other clubs to acquire what we can, and then we go back to our own club. Imagine my surprise when I saw Sera with none other than my fake-ass Prez's son. I let my real brother in on what I saw, and he took it from there. I got to stay put to get information and he took care of shit on the outside. It was the perfect plan, actually."

"Shit, that is a perfect plan."

I hear rustling, my gaze flying toward where Joker disappeared. In his place, I find Twist creeping steadily and quietly toward us. Fuck, I hope Capone doesn't see him. "Say, Capone, what happened to Seraphina?"

"Oh, that bitch took off. Joker said we should make her be a club slut after the shit she pulled. I reckon she found out. She comes home, though, and we'll have our fun with her."

Twist stares at my face and I shake my head as much as I can, I make a shooing motion with my hand. I hope he sees my movements.

Twist glares and shakes his head in return. Fuck, why is he being tenacious? If Joker walks up behind him, then he's fucked. I watch him as far as I can without turning my head as he scales the outer perimeter of the barn.

"Do you think Seraphina could be with Brently?"

I wonder if he's hiding her to keep her safe. I've never seen or met her, but Brently must be pretty hung up on her to keep dealing with this shit. I'm glad Avery doesn't have two psycho brothers out to get me.

There's a gurgle and I no longer feel the gun at my back so I quickly turn around.

Twist stands in front of me holding his large hunting knife that drips with blood. He's relaxed, as if the kill was rejuvenating for him. On the floor, Capone lies holding his neck, gasping for air as blood sputters from the large gash across his throat. His eyes bug and dark liquid coats his hands, pooling under him as the life drains out of his irises.

"There's another," I whisper, and Twist shakes his head.

"No, he's knocked out and tied up back behind all the farming equipment."

"How did you know?"

"When we got here I walked behind the barn to take a piss and saw the missing boards. I decided to climb through and check it out. The brothers said you'd come in, so I figured if anything I'd try to make you jump."

I meet his gaze, humbly. I don't know how to repay him for saving my life and quite possibly all the brothers' lives. "Thank you, brother," I murmur genuinely and reach my hand out.

He shakes it and slaps my back with his free hand, "Anytime, brother."

We trek to the barn door and I use a cinder block to prop it open. At this point I can't wait to kill all these assholes after hearing what kind of people they really are.

Avery

It's morning and they still aren't back. I'd reached over to feel 2's muscular body this morning and was met with cold sheets. I really don't know what to think.

Did they go out and he met someone new? I hate feeling as if I'm not adequate enough for him. I think it comes from how my mother's pushed me to do better my entire life.

I think I learned that in Psych 101, my second year of college. I wonder what a shrink would say about my mother's insane need to be in control of everything?

Brushing my teeth, I flip on shower. May as well clean up and get dressed, otherwise, I'll just lie in bed and let my mind run rampant with thoughts if I don't do something. This is a prime example of why I don't get serious with anyone. I can't turn off my thoughts, and I waste my time thinking about a million possible scenarios.

Stepping into the shower, the hot water beats down on my shoulders and back. *So refreshing.* I can't help but reminisce about the last time I was in here and 2 joined me. I loved it when he bent me over and bit into my back.

I wonder how it'd have been with Ares in here with us as well. Would he have been in control like he was the other night? It seems they complement each other so well. They were in sync and made me feel wonderful.

I hope we get to do that again and even more. I wish they'd have woken me up to finish what they'd started. I'll never forget rousing awake to find Ares standing there with his large, exposed cock, hungry for a taste of me. I'd never really fantasized about being with two men before, and now I can't seem to stop. Both of them made me feel wanted and adored.

Leaning my head back against the shower wall, I close my eyes letting my imagination run loose. I picture 2 biting into my neck and Ares wrapping my hair in his fist, giving it a light tug. My palms skim over my hard nipples, reminiscing about 2. He'd smothered my breasts with his mouth, drawing my buds in through the raspy material of his shirt I was wearing. I'd felt as if I was going to orgasm from them playing with my breasts alone.

My hand falls lower, brushing the smooth skin of my stomach until I reach my core. Pushing my finger into my wet center I imagine it's one of Ares' long fingers pumping in and out of me. The water trickles down and it's almost as if a tongue is licking, caressing all over my hypersensitive skin.

Picturing Ares behind me, he holds me tight against his chest and reaches around, busily thrusting his fingers in and out. 2 Piece would be in front of me biting and nibbling all over my body. He'd eventually make his way downward to suck on my swollen clit as Ares continually pumps into me deeply.

I grip the shower wall tighter, holding on with my free hand as my pussy spasms. It clenches around my finger as a rush of mind-numbing sensations wash over my body. IT's enough that I moan, coming, wishing I wasn't in here alone.

It's lunchtime and I'm starving so I go on the hunt for some food. I poke my head in the dining room. I've always thought it was magical how food just pops up in this dining area. I asked 2 if they have a cook that hides away so I never see them.

According to him, they have a few club whores who enjoy cooking. They make food whenever they feel like it and put it out on the long dining table for everyone to pick at. I'm not fond of the whole club whore aspect, but I am cool with having food cooked and waiting for me whenever I get hungry.

The room's empty except for a solitary figure eating with his back to me and staring out the window. "Come sit and eat, sweetheart," he grunts, and I jump.

Guess I'm not as quiet as I like to believe I am. His long, blond hair reaches his shoulders, and his arms are fully covered in colorful tattoos. He's not a big man, but decent size and very striking for being a bit older.

"I thought that was you. You don't mind my company?"

He's always kind to me, but I don't want to presume he's not dealing with his own crap. Being President of an MC must be extremely stressful especially with his son showing up mutilated.

"No, get yourself some food and come pop a squat."

That makes me chuckle. These broody bikers do have a sense of humor. It's amazing how you can get a bunch of grown men together and they act like kids sometimes.

"Sounds like a plan."

Fixing my plate with some pancakes and tons of butter and syrup, I sit next to him. There's definitely an appeal to eating in front of the window. You can take in the grassy land and trees like a little bit of peace in a world of chaos.

"How are you today?" I turn toward him and gaze over his handsome features up close.

Geez, how is he not married, with like fifteen kids running around, being that gorgeous?

It makes me think of all the weird stepbrother/daddy books I've seen lately. I get it now, because if Prez was my stepdaddy, I'd be panting for him. I'd damn sure call him daddy and offer to be his good girl. God, I'm messed up, but damn, some fantasy.

"Ah, I'm all right, how 'bout yourself?" He peers over at me with soft greyish-blue irises.

I take in his short beard and weathered lines around his eyes. You wouldn't notice them unless you were close enough. He always seems so serious too, as if he has the weight of the world on his shoulders.

"I'm okay." Shrugging, I pick at my food, chewing on the inside of my lip.

"Relax, sweetheart, 2 is just fine," he mutters, and I perk up, hopeful.

"You've heard from him?"

"No. I did hear from Ares though. They're handling club business. Just keep your chin up, girl. You'll be straight and fit in around here. He'll be back when he's done and he'll be looking for you."

Nodding, I take a bite then sigh, "Sweet Jesus, y'all have some good cooks here."

"That we do, girl, that we do." He chuckles and we finish our meal in comfortable silence.

I can see the appeal Prez had to 2 Piece. He seems to know more than he should for his age, but doesn't advertise it. I bet this man would be very interesting if you could get him to open up.

Smiling, I squeeze his forearm gently as I stand up to throw my stuff in the trash. I turn to leave when he clears his throat and I meet his gaze.

"It's nice having some new females around here and some kids. I hope you'll stick around."

"If he asks, I may do that."

He smirks and nods. I grin back at him and head out. I'm going to check out the bar and see if I can hunt down London's sexy ass.

2 Piece

About eight hours later...

I'm exhausted and ready to get back to the clubhouse, but we haven't even gotten started yet. We unloaded all the nasty Twisted Snakes and have them tied up securely in the barn. It's taken hours for the gas to wear off for some of them.

Twist and I recounted to the brothers everything that happened with Capone and Joker. Ares said it was best to not discuss it here. He thinks we need to wait until we get in church and to talk to Prez.

We've basically been sitting here with our thumbs up our asses all night. The brothers seem at a loss, fighting with their thoughts and feelings about Capone. We were completely blindsided and it's made everyone feel like a giant fool.

The brothers seem more agitated and ready to take some anger out on the Snakes. Nobody likes a traitor and when you form a bond with that person, you're bound to feel a sense of betrayal. I'm sure each of us have our own ideas on what we'd like to do to him for this.

At least the bullshit between Twist and me seems to be resolved. I hate fighting with my brothers. It's been on replay in my mind all night; I still can't get over that whole shit with Capone. The fact I never noticed anything makes me wonder what else I've been blind to.

"You coming, bro?" Cain stands in front of me with a guy thrown over his shoulder.

"Yeah, what are you going to do with that one?"

"This one's for you," he offers jovially.

I shake my head and grit, "I want to deal with Joker. I have a bone to pick with him."

"All right, cool, man. I'll toss this one to Spin. I think he's the one that tatted up Brently anyhow. See if Spin can get creative with a fellow inker."

Guess it's time to show these assholes what happens when you fuck with other people's lives. I watch as Ares grips the Twisted Snake's President's wrist then slams his boot down to snap the man's bone. The President screams desperately and it reverberates throughout the barn.

"You hurt my Prez's kid. It's my job to see you get the correct punishment. Life is full of choices and balance. You made the decision to allow your peons to brutalize another human being. Welcome to hell, motherfucker," Ares snarls and snaps another bone.

I don't know how he can handle feeling another's bones break as he holds them. It gives me chills all over. I hold my breath; just the noise and frantic screams coming from the man shriveled at Ares' feet are making me want to gag.

"You coming?" Cain whistles and waves his hand in front of my face. I blink. Then attempt to shake off the image fresh in my head of that last snap, as well as the composed features of Ares as he performed his task.

Drawing in a deep breath, I comply, "Yeah, man, let's do this."

Following him through the barn, he throws the man off his shoulder in front of Spin. Spin rolls his eyes and the piece of shit on the floor begins his first round of pleading. He's in for some fun.

I make my way behind Cain to where Joker's tied up in the center of the barn. He glares spitefully as I get closer.

"You angry because Twist killed your brother dearest?" He remains silent, so I shrug. No skin off my back if he decides to stay quiet. "You know, I think those hogs out back could motivate you to talk." I chortle, and Cain chuckles beside me.

Chin-lifting towards Joker's legs, I motion for him to help. Cain grabs the right leg while I grab the left. We trek for the hogs, dragging Joker behind us.

He's a stubborn fuck not even making a peep. I'd think he'd at least squirm and attempt to make it hard for me. It's almost as if he's pouting and attempting to ignore us.

Stupid fucker.

We approach the hogs and a few squeal in excitement as they see us. They've gotten used to the brothers dropping off *food*. Who knew hogs were carnivores. I always thought they ate slop and veggies. "Yeah, yeah, fuckers, we got ya' a snack!" I call out.

Cain grins evilly and it makes me sick to my stomach, imagining what's about to happen to this lowlife piece of shit. I know he deserves his fate, but I'm not into torturing fools either. We toss his legs down next to the wooden pig pen.

"Anything you want to say? Maybe apologize for fucking with my girl and my club." I scowl at him as he lies in the dirt.

He snarls and spits toward me.

"Well, you done fucked up with that one." I shake my head, chastising him and glance over at Cain's amused expression, sighing loudly. "All right, brother, let's see if the hogs will get him talking and confessing his wrong doings."

"Sounds good, man." He snatches both of Joker's legs. I wrap my arm around his neck in a choke hold and we lift him over the fence into the hogs' chow trough.

The hogs move as quickly as they can, to be the first for dinner. Grabbing the bucket next to the gate that's filled with leftover slop, I pour it all over Joker's body as evenly as I can. The pigs swarm him and start to feast on their treat.

Joker's body jerks violently as he attempts to turn away from the hungry, plump beasts. They grunt and squeak as they start to rip his clothes to shreds and get their first taste of flesh. Joker's pupils widen immensely as he opens his mouth to let loose a horrific spine-tingling yell.

I'd normally turn away for something gruesome like this, but not today. I'm going to watch the entire thing, because Avery deserves that revenge, and Brently deserves his vengeance. Like Ares said, life is full of choices. This fucker just made the wrong choice, with the wrong person.

Avery might not realize it yet, but when it comes to her safety I'd kill for her—any day. However, after the horrendous act I've just committed, I no longer believe I can look her in the eyes and feel adequate for her. I'm tainted, stained, and sullied; I know it, and she will soon if I'm around her enough.

I've always been fucked up, but this takes it to a new level. I have no remorse for the individual I just heaved to his death. I should feel something if I'm a decent person, shouldn't I? Clearly, I'm not and Avery deserves someone who can give her everything she warrants in life. She doesn't deserve a killer.

I hear the shriek of the miter saw fire up inside the barn and turn to Cain. He just shrugs and swaggers toward the barn. Glancing back, the pigs are busy working diligently on the mutilated pieces of leftover body in their feeding trough. Their faces are covered in blood and gore; it's sickening but gives me a sense of closure. *Well, he's obviously dead.*

Cain enters the barn and I follow along, immediately wishing with every fiber of my being that I hadn't. Inside, Ares stands behind the loud, screeching miter saw. He has a black rubber apron on over his clothes and bears the part of a real life psychopath, chopping up various body parts of the Snakes.

Twist diligently assists and it takes my full concentration not to puke everywhere. I wasn't cut out for this. I've felt sick with each turn of events today.

Nightmare and Exterminator stand with the Twisted Snakes' President. His body's beaten with its limbs tweaked in odd angles. It's Ares' handiwork no doubt. It's amazing how he calms himself now and doesn't black out when he sets out to destroy his prey.

The President's barely alive, covered in piss, bruises, and blood. Any man would've pissed himself with Ares in charge of torture and behind a saw. Well, maybe not Nightmare; that dude's fucking intimidating as hell. I can't even fathom the thoughts that'd run rampant through Avery and London's heads were they to find us in this situation.

"Bring him here," Ares orders Ex and Night. They snatch up the Prez and carry him toward the beat-up wooden bench, where the miter saw is bolted down. Now, instead of it being caked with aged wood dust, it's thoroughly coated in dark syrupy blood.

The Prez grunts, his eyes widening as they close in on the table. *I can't see this shit.* I turn and exit the barn quickly; I don't know how he does it.

Fuck that shit. I'm a little crazy, sure, but that's pure fucked up shit back there. Feeding the hogs was bad enough, but holding someone and cutting them in pieces while they're still alive takes the cake for me.

I make it to the side of the barn before the sandwich I had for dinner last night makes it's reappearance. Jumping back, I move so it doesn't get on my boots, and then wipe the tears that run down the side of my face as I puke. I don't know why, but ever since I was a kid, my eyes leak if I get sick.

When I was little, Mom used to tell me it was my tummy weeping because it hurt. Stupid bitch had to go and turn to shit. I'll never feel whole inside because of all that bullshit growing up.

"All done, brother, we can head back to the club. The rest are going to handle the mess inside and feed the porkers their dinner," Cain mutters, and claps me on the back.

I swear if we ever have a hog roast, I won't be eating those fucking pigs.

Cain and I load up in Loretta and go back to the club, eager to get the hell out of there. I scan the room for Avery when we arrive, even though I know I need to talk to Prez first. I can't believe everything that went down. My mind is still reeling.

Smiles' chilling at the bar, drinking a cold beer. My mouth salivates as I watch the condensation drop along the side of the bottle. He's been quiet lately. I wonder what that's about.

Fuck, I really don't want to be the one to fill Prez in about Capone. Smiles chin-lifts toward me and I return the gesture. The benefit of being a biker, we don't need many words to convey our messages. Cain's ass is a talker but most of us like to keep more of our shit inside.

Brently's posted up on the coach, same place we left him.

"'Sup, kid, where's your pops?" I glance over his stomach as I ask. Poor guy, he got fucked up. I'd be pissed if that shit happened to me.

"Dad's in his office." He gestures toward the hall.

"Thanks." I head that way and rap a few times on the half-open door.

Prez glances up from his paper on his desk. He looks me over, his eyes calculating. "2? Brother, you straight?" He relaxes back in his beat-up office chair and steeples his fingers in front of his chest.

"Yeah, Prez, mind if I take a seat?" I gesture to the couch resting against the wall. Might as well be at a goddamn shrink's office, I know that's about how this'll play out. With me confessing everything to him and not feeling any better when I leave.

He nods and I sit on the edge of a cushion, propping my elbows on my knees, leaning forward. Best to get this out quickly then I can go hunt down Avery. I proceed to tell him everything that went down, all the way from when we first arrived at the Twisted Snakes' compound. I get to the altercation with Capone, and his mouth visibly tightens yet he remains silent until I complete my recount of events.

Once I finish, I sit further into the cushions and lean my head back. I'm exhausted and stressed out. I hate being tense; it makes me get the itch to leave on a run.

"Fuck, I knew he was jealous of you, but even *I* had no idea he had that up his sleeve. Goddamn traitor, I can't stand rats! If that's the case, then y'all did the right thing," He reassures.

"I'm sick of all this bullshit." I rub my hands over my eyes and the scruff warming my jaw.

"Stop stressing, 2. It's all figured out now; the Snakes are gone and you can chill with your girl for a while."

"Ha, my girl? She isn't my fucking girl. She's nothing to me. She can't and shouldn't handle this shit," I scowl.

I hear a hiccup and quickly turn toward the door. Avery's standing there with tears trailing down her cheeks. Fuck, that came out wrong and she heard it. Prez glares at me and shakes his head. Avery shoots me a heartbroken expression and takes off quickly from the doorway. Fuck, she must have been watching for me to come back.

"Go fix that shit, son; that's a good one and you just about fucked it all up." He points angrily at me and I stand.

Fuck, how am I going to fix this? Maybe I should let her go.

I look at Prez and shake my head. "Nah, man, she deserves better than me. I'm too screwed up for her. I want her to have a decent life, not be worried about getting shot or about me going to jail and shit." I shrug, my mind made up and glance toward the door again as if she'd still be there, only she's gone.

"Listen to me, and you listen good, son. I know what you're doing right now. I know, because I did that same shit to my wife and kids. Worst damn mistake of my entire life. You though, you have a chance to fix it before it's too late."

"I can't mend that shit. Besides, what's she going to do with someone like me- someone who's broken?"

"You idiot, you're just lazy and scared. Everyone's broken in some way; you just have to see if your broken pieces fit together. Now get the fuck out of my office."

Throwing up the deuces, I walk to my room. He doesn't have to tell me twice. Shit, he'd probably end up shooting me to get his point across.

Opening my door, I'm met with the heartbreaking sounds of sobs coming from the woman I've grown to adore. When did I fall for her? It's like it just happened when I wasn't paying attention, and now I've gone and messed up. I'm rotten for her anyhow. I have to keep chanting that to myself, as I make my way inside.

Breezing over her puffy pink face that's swollen from her tears, I swallow, attempting to ease the sudden dryness. I've never been one to deal with chicks, so I have no idea what to do or say here. Thankfully, my sister turned out to be quite the ballbuster so I didn't have to experience any emotional breakdowns. If she did have them, then she hid them extremely well.

Avery's ember irises scan me from head to toe as she stuffs clothes into her bag. Her tear-kissed eyelashes make me want to pull her to me and hold her until they disappear.

I clear my throat and slowly make my way into the center of the room. She sniffles and stares at me as if she's waiting for me to speak. I don't know what the fuck to say to her though.

After a few beats, I notice the disappointment cloud her eyes and she throws her belongings into her bag quicker. She bustles into the bathroom and the little clinks of her swiping her makeup off the counter into her bag echoes throughout the room. This seems final, like this is it and makes me feel even worse inside than I did back at the barn. How can losing her appear more tragic than torturing and killing people?

She comes storming out of the room and I sidestep in front of her. I don't know what to say, but I have to say something. I'm afraid if I don't, this sensation in my gut won't disappear.

"It came out wrong," I whisper and watch for her reaction.

She tilts her head, thoughtful for a second, "Which part?" She hiccups and looks at the ground.

Fuck, I'm such a bastard.

"All of it. I meant it as if, you deserve better, not someone like me." I tilt her chin up gently with my pointer and middle fingers.

She finally meets my eyes and it breaks something inside me to witness her so distraught. I just killed someone for upsetting her, yet here I am making her cry for me. "I don't want someone else; I want you." Her lips quiver and I take in her puffy mouth. It's swollen from her crying, when it should only be that way from my kisses.

Leaning in a touch closer, I breathe her in. My nose is inches from hers and I stare longingly at her mouth. I could have it, that mouth, those lips; she could be all mine if I choose. I breathe out and her lashes flutter closed.

Nudging her nose with mine, she bites down on her bottom lip. I grasp her hip and tug her body to mine, watching as she patiently waits for me to make my move. She's giving herself to me right now, mine for the taking, exposed and vulnerable. I never thought the notion of a woman completely submitting herself over would be such a fucking turn on.

Grasping her cheek with my other hand, I tilt her face where I want it. "Look at me, Avery," I command, and she opens her eyes lazily, taking in my expression.

She wants me to control her, needs me to dominate her. I use my thumb to release her lip and take it with my own mouth. Drawing it into my mouth, she releases a moan.

Pulling back, I gaze at her, serious. "Undress yourself for me. I want to see all of you."

She complies, removing her shirt to reveal a plain black lacy bra. It doesn't faze me however. I'm an ass man, and Avery's all ass.

"Take off your pants."

She unbuttons the clasp and pushes them off, kicking the material off to the side.

"Turn around and bend over. Hold onto your ankles," I command, and she does as she's told, keeping silent, following my directions precisely.

Her ass is fully on display in front of me, only covered by a miniscule thong. Using my index finger, I push the fabric out of the way so I can see her glistening sex. It saturates the meager fabric with her excitement. I clench my other hand, struggling not to lose control and just take her like a wild animal, rutting for my satisfaction only.

"Very good, now stand up and take your panties off before I rip them." She does as she's told, still facing away so her ass is in front of me. "Next time I'll call for Ares, but right now, you are only mine. Understand?"

Shorty nods and I smack her ass sharply. She hisses out between her teeth, "*Yes.*"

"Get on your hands and knees, on the bed."

I can't believe how incredibly beautiful she is like this. She wants to be mine, well then; I'm going to fuck her as if she's mine. Standing behind her, I push my fingers into her soft, wet center. She easily coats them and it's so fucking sexy. She's as turned on as I am, if not more.

I unbutton my pants and quickly shove them down, then pull her hips to me. Slamming inside her, it's brutal. This isn't fucking around, I'm taking her. Reaching for my hem I shuck my shirt and toss it on the floor.

225

"Ah," she calls on impact, and I pump into her savagely again. She'll still feel me, long after this is over with.

Avery utters a brief grunt with each thrust and I softly skim my fingers over her tummy until I reach her clit. Clasping the nub between my two fingers, I lightly pinch it, over and over.

"Oh- 2, oh!" she moans. It's loud as her hips begin to move with my fingers. She grinds her ass into me, and my balls tighten up at the sensation.

Releasing her clit, I run my hand up over her perky tits, tweaking her nipples as I go. I don't stop until my palms firmly wrapped around her throat. I pull her back into my chest until she has to hold onto the footboard with one hand and reach behind her to grasp my hip.

Flexing my fingers tightly around her neck, I pump inside her, thrusting deep. She attempts to moan again, but I choke it back with my fingers, squeezing and applying pressure each time.

"You shut that tempting, little fucking mouth, Avery. If I want you to speak, I will tell you to fucking talk. I'm taking you- you're mine right now."

She nods her head shortly, complying and I grip her hips harder as I thrust inside her wetness.

God, she feels so good; she pleases me to no end with each plunge I take.

Her chest constricts against my forearm, her scream attempting to break free as I cut of her oxygen again and again. My mouth finds her neck, sucking, claiming, marking the woman who's become mine in a blink of an eye and she gives in to me even more. Her pussy walls clamp down like a vice around my engorged cock, breaking my hold and letting her moan loose.

The sexy rasp in her moan does me in. My cock throbs so desperately, begging for permission to release my cum inside her that I bite down, leaving my mark on the crevice where her shoulder meets her neck. As I nibble and play with the skin making it a deep red, I release my thick seed inside her sweet tightness. The orgasm is powerful, as I concentrate on how much she means to me. It goes on far longer than any I've experienced prior, solidifying my evolving feelings.

Lazily, afterwards, I skim my hand down the flesh of her throat, hooking her waist to pull her on the bed to lie beside me. She keeps her back to me as I play with her hair until I doze off into a restless nap. I'm so damn tired from being up all night; I can't help but find comfort in the warmth from the woman who owns my heart.

Wow.

I didn't see things ending up like that. I thought after hearing him in the office, we were done with. I'm glad I waited before calling Niko this time. He would've freaked and probably killed 2 Piece.

I feel like an emotional, crazy woman with him all the time. I wish he'd be up front and tell me. Hell, spell it out what he wants and feels.

Right when we take a step forward it seems like we get thrown backward. We just had earth shattering sex; he said he was taking me as his. Was that literally, me being his now, or just in the moment?

Ugh.

I hate being this confused. I need to just buckle down and discuss it with him. We also need to talk about him being gone for so long. I was worried sick and he didn't even call me. If we're going to work and be a couple I need to set up some boundaries or guidelines or...something.

"2?" I whisper. I don't know why I'm whispering, but for some reason it feels wrong to break the comfortable silence we are sharing.

Hmm, I don't get an answer. "Umm, 2?" I repeat louder but again, get nothing.

What the hell.

Peeking over my shoulder, I find him wearing the most peaceful, sweetest expression and he's fast asleep. His lips are parted slightly and with each exhale his bottom lip trembles.

His face appears younger when he's sleeping and not busy worrying or contemplating a million different things.

He has beautiful, long eyelashes that any woman would envy, but I'd never tell him that. He'd think it's too unmanly, when in reality it complements his gorgeous eyes. His face is extra scruffy, but still as handsome as ever.

Reaching out, I run the tips of my fingers lightly through his beard and over his cheekbones. He has a proud nose and soft skin on his cheeks even though they're a little weathered from riding. The contrast of our skin tone stands out as I take in his rich tan and my pale fingertips.

I don't even know his name. How can I be this gone over someone whose real name I don't know? Staring at him in this moment, I'm certain I'm done for.

I'm crazy about him. He's infuriating and confusing but also amazing and consuming. I feel like I'm being pulled in a thousand directions when it comes to him.

Is it the right choice to stick around? I overheard all those hurtful things he said in the office but then he tells me he didn't mean it like it sounded. Yet men say we women are the confusing ones. He doesn't know it yet, but I do plan to keep him. When we're finally able to hash everything out, I hope he's okay with that.

We both like our freedom and not being tied to anything, I guess we're kind of like wanderers. That must mean we're kindred spirits, right? I'm ready to relinquish that sense of freedom though and be 'free' with him, together. I just pray he's ready to as well.

There's a knock on the bedroom door and it stirs me out of my thoughts of my future with the man I care about. I glance over at the door, waiting to see if it was indeed this door. I chew on my lip, staring.

Yep, definitely a knock. I think as they rap on the door again. Damn it, I'm pretty comfy and don't really feel like shifting from this position. I know if it's Niko, though, he'll start beating away on the wood and 2 Piece obviously needs his rest. He must be tuckered out since he dozed off—without even a word—right after we were intimate.

Crawling out of bed, I attempt to not jostle the mattress too much and disturb him. Snatching up his shirt off the floor, I throw it on and make my way to answer the door.

Only it's not a big, burly, blond Russian waiting for me; it's a tiny female version of 2 Piece. She's gorgeous with blonde hair and sun-kissed cheeks. She props her hand on her hip and looks at me from the tips of my toes to the top of my head.

Since she's doing some inspecting, I return the favor and notice this little chica has a big round belly. Hmm, 2 hasn't said anything about dear old sister being prego, so this could be awkward.

"Hi," I greet quietly and offer up a small smile.

She's a little hesitant at first but then returns my smile, "Hi, is my brother in there?"

"Yes, ma'am; he's asleep though. Is he expecting you?"

"No, he didn't know I was coming. I just made a quick decision and headed down." She fidgets with her shirt and blushes a little.

"You're from Cali, right?"

She smiles bigger this time and nods. "He's told you about me?" she asks, surprised.

"Yes, but not a lot, just he has a sister in Cali. I'm Avery, his, umm…friend," I mutter, nervously and stick my hand out like a dork.

I can't believe I'm meeting his family right now. Besides the brothers, she's his only family, so this is kind of a big deal. At least it is to me. I hope one day he can meet my family too.

She giggles softly and shakes my hand. Great, she probably thinks I'm a goober.

"You find him, baby?" Twist asks as he walks down the hall toward us. She gets a shy look and nods at him.

Oh my, looks like Twist may have an admirer. 2 would probably slaughter Twist if he knew his sister was crushing.

He smirks down at her, and, for the first time, I notice Twist has a dimple just like Cain. He may have more but right now I can only see the one. "Cool, how about you come and take it easy, sugar pie. Don't want you hurting after such a long drive." He places his arm over her shoulder and she beams up at him.

"Okay, Avery, will you please tell my brother I'm here when he wakes? I tried calling him a couple of times during my trip down here, but he never answered."

"Sure, I definitely will. It was nice to meet you, umm..."

"Oh yes, I'm Sadie," she replies, clearly surprised that she forgot to say her name.

"I thought so, just wasn't completely sure."

She grins. "Yep, that's me."

Her and Twist leave, going toward the main room and I can't help but think they're cute like that. This' going to be interesting. I'm keeping my mouth shut over the looks I just witnessed too. I don't want to get in the middle of something that could be brewing.

Heading back in to the room, I shut the door behind me. I may as well get dressed. I'm not tired and I'm sure Niko will be floating around here somewhere. I cover 2 up with the blue fleece throw from the end of the bed and head to the bathroom to take a shower.

When I open the bathroom door, 2 Piece is sitting up in bed with his hair wild. It's short, but it still gets a bedhead tussled appearance. I love when he has that just woken up, sleepy look on his face. He's adorable and is always a bit disoriented for a few minutes. It's one of the very few times you get to witness him as vulnerable.

"Hey, free bird," he rasps, my insides clench from that deep, gruff sound.

"Well, don't you just look yummy. So, did you sleep well? You were so tired."

He chuckles and the timbre of his laugh makes me sigh in bliss. What is it about a man's voice that can turn us to mush?

"Yeah, I'm feeling better; pussy, sleep and then your fine ass. I'm perfect, Shorty. I need to take a shower though."

"Okay, well we had a visitor probably forty or so minutes ago. Your sister is here. She asked me to tell you when you woke up."

"Sadie? Oh shit, was she okay?"

"Yeah, she seemed fine. Twist was showing her around and talking to her while you were sleeping."

"All right, then let me shower really quick and maybe we can all grab some grub or something?"

"Sure, sounds good." I smile and he grins back at me as he enters the bathroom.

Well, at least he seems to be in a better mood now. I think I'm going to paint my toes pink while I wait for him to get done.

A few minutes later he comes out with a billow of steam surrounding his stark-naked ass. Reel yourself in, woman; do not jump him like you want to. He has to see his sister and we need to have a serious discussion over absolutely everything. No getting distracted again by sex.

He puts on his boxer briefs. Damn, is it possible for his ass to look even better in his underwear? He pivots slightly as he bends to grab his jeans.

Yep, definitely possible.

He pulls on a pair of clean jeans, a plain white T-shirt and his cut. He catches me staring and clicks his tongue at me. "Later, Shorty, control yourself," he teases, shaking his head.

"Whatever, you know you want to call Ares to come play," I retort saucily.

His eyes widen with anticipation. "Fucking right I do, but first I have to see why Sadie's shown up out of the blue."

I nod and put my nail polish back in my bag.

"You don't have to keep stuffing your shit away in your suitcase either. Leave it wherever you want to, Shorty," he says and I get the deer-in-the-headlights kind of stare going on. "It's cool; we'll take it slow, 'kay?"

"Yeah, I wanted to discuss a few things with you."

"I know, but we'll have to get to it later," he says stubbornly and I grit my teeth to not argue with him.

I understand he's distracted by his sister, but he better not put me on the backburner now and use this as an excuse to not get this situated. I nod and make my way out the door with him. I will not let this go. Next time we're alone, we're talking.

2 Piece

Avery and I get to the main room and the first thing I hear is Sadie arguing with London. Her shrill voice when she gets angry could stand out to me in a crowd full of people. She's a fucking ballbuster and London's a wildcat; shit could pop off in a split second.

I have no idea what they could possibly be arguing about. Those two don't even know each other. It has to stop quickly though, or Prez will be looking to throw somebody out. I don't want to brawl with Cain's crazy ass over shit between my sister and his ol' lady, either.

We arrive to chaos erupting. Cain's standing in front of London while Twist stands in front of Sadie. The girls scream back and forth at each other. London looks ready to murder my sister and Sadie just looks annoyed.

"Bitch, I will smoke your ass like grass!" London screams.

"Fuck you, crazy heifer; you're psycho!"

"I am fucking psycho, you pip-squeak! Don't you forget it next time you look at my man."

"I wasn't looking at your man, for Christ's sake; I was talking to Twist and you decided to flip out."

"Yeah, because you were staring at Cain. Newsflash, bitch, he belongs to me."

"I wasn't staring at him like that. I was staring because he looked familiar."

"Sure, that's what all the whores say. I don't care if you fucked him in the past. He's *not* interested."

"I never fucked him. He looks like my brother's friend, you twat face!" my sister screeches in return.

I have to stop this; it's ridiculous.

"Woah," I placate with my hands out in calm down motions. I feel like I'm walking into a hornet's nest.

"London, this is my younger sister, Sadie. She probably saw Cain when I first met him in Cali."

"I don't care who she is; just stay the fuck away from my ol' man." She scowls and Cain chuckles jovially. He loves London getting all territorial, means they'll go fuck like crazy afterward. He once told me that's when they have the best sex and he can talk her into trying to get knocked up again.

"Trust me; I'm fucking six months pregnant. I'm not looking to get another piece-of-shit man."

I'm sorry, what did she just say? I nearly get whiplash from turning so quickly, trying to see her belly. It's kind of, if I can't see it, then it can't be real sort of scenario.

How the fuck is she pregnant? Last time I was there I didn't see a man coming around at all. She has some serious explaining to do.

"The fuck you say, Sadie?" I growl, flabbergasted.

"You heard me, Silas, I'm having a baby," she replies tartly, and Avery draws in a breath beside to me. I glance at her quickly and see she's surprised. I have no idea why, but I'm sure she'll be filling me in later.

"Sadie, how the fuck did you get pregnant?"

Cain chuckles behind me, attempting to coax London to go to his club room. I knew it; the fucker's going to have her knocked up again by tomorrow.

"I'd go with the old-fashioned way; but do you want me to give you the details?"

"Gross, Sades." I turn back to Avery and point at her. "Don't drink the water or whatever the fuck's getting people pregnant."

She holds her hands up and smiles. "No way, I'm very careful about that type of thing."

I roll my eyes at Sadie. I'm pissed, but trying to stay calm. What can you do in this situation but show your support. She's still my baby sister and I just want to know who the guilty fucker is, so I can go kill him.

"Look, Silas, it's done and there is nothing we can do about it. I didn't come here for you to freak out on me, but because I needed to be around my family during all these changes."

"I know, kid. You just blindsided me on this shit. I mean, why didn't you tell me sooner or something?" I grumble, my anger beginning to dissipate, when I get a good look at her.

She seems so damn beat down and tired. I've never witnessed my sister stressed out. She always takes everything with a grain of salt and rolls with whatever's thrown at her. Right now, she's frail with a big belly sticking out.

"I was scared to tell you sooner. I wasn't sure of what was happening and stuff." She moves away from Twist and sits at the bar. He posts up next to her, and I have to stop myself from growling at him. He did save my life in that barn and he also helped keep my sister safe a few minutes ago.

Sadie's feisty but London could seriously hurt someone if she gets pissed enough. I think Cain's been teaching her some techniques; not that she needed it in the first place. London's like a princess around here with the brothers, and it could make Sadie's life harder if London doesn't like her. We've never met the real club princess, Prez's girl; not sure if we ever will.

I sit on the other side of her and pull Avery to stand in between my legs so she can be a part of the conversation. "Sades, this is my chick, Avery." I nod toward Avery and she beams a kind smile at my sister.

"Yeah, we met when I came to your room."

"That's right, my bad. Oh well. So, we thought maybe you'd want to get some food. Are you hungry?"

"Not really, Twist was kind enough to get me some food and a drink when I got here." She fidgets as she says this and my eyes find Twist's.

He sits there gloating like a proud fucker, yet he knows I can't get angry at him for making sure she was taken care of and fed. Damn it, do I want to though. Fucker's cozying right the fuck on up to my sister and she's pregnant. What could he possibly get out of this with my sister and her kid?

"All right. So, who's responsible for knocking you up?" Might as well ask the question I really want to know. Looks like I may be making a run out to Cali to hunt down the assclown that touched my sister but was too much of a pussy to come and meet me himself.

"Just some guy, it doesn't matter." She glances down and it pisses me off again.

When the hell did she become so meek? It's only been months since I saw her. What could possibly have happened in that short period of time?

"Yes, Sadie, it fucking matters, now give me a goddamn name."

Her lip trembles slightly. "No, Silas, it doesn't matter. He's gone okay?" she argues, bringing some color to her cheeks again.

"What the hell do you mean, 'he's gone'? Where did he go?"

"I mean he's gone. As in, he took off. He fucking left me, okay?"

"No, it's not okay. Tell me his name and we'll find him," I promise her, in full-on protective big brother mode. I'll run this dude down and put a hurtin' on him for messing with my sister.

Her big blue eyes pool with tears and they stream down her cheeks when she blinks. She sniffles in a breath. "That's just it. He's gone. He doesn't exist. He didn't even give me his real name when we were seeing each other. I've searched. You don't think I'd look for him? It's all I've been doing for months. Why do you think it took me so long to come to you? I was ashamed."

She sniffles abruptly, taking a deep breath. "I'm ashamed, I'm embarrassed, and I don't know what to do now. I'm scared, Silas, he's gone and I'm left with this little baby all by myself. I can't believe this happened to me. Why do they always leave, Silas? Am I so horrible they all have to leave?" She starts to sob, and Twist pulls her into his chest to comfort her.

He talks soothingly into her hair as he embraces her tightly. "Shush, sugar pie. It'll all be okay; don't you worry about a thing. You need to calm down though, baby. It's not good, you getting upset so much."

Staring at her, my heart hurts badly; it feels as if it could burst. This all stems back to my father. That piece of shit left and she has always blamed herself. I swear to God if I ever find this fuckwad, he'll pay for doing this to her.

I'll let Twist hold her. She needs a man to be strong for her right now. I'll be that for her, but I know my brothers will help also. Twist chin-lifts to me and I raise my eyebrows.

"Let me get her settled in a guest room and we can talk later about what to do about everything," Twist mutters, and I bite the inside of my cheek hoping the shot of pain will calm my restlessness.

I'm telling myself not to just hop on my bike right now and drive up and down every single street in my hometown to search for this creep. "She doesn't need this sort of stress with her baby and all. She needs to rest for a while," he tries to reason with me.

"Yeah, I guess that's a good idea; thanks, brother." I nod at him, then lean in closer and tenderly kiss Sadie on her forehead. "Go relax, Sades, we'll figure this all out later, okay?"

She glances at me sorrowfully and mumbles "Thanks." Twist leads her towards the spare rooms.

What the fuck am I going to do about this shit? Fuck.

Avery hugs me tighter around my torso and I concentrate on her for the first time since we came to the bar. "It'll be okay, 2, you'll figure something out. I'll help any way you need me to."

I smile down at her. She's so amazing and I can't believe I almost pushed her away. I lean in and kiss her tenderly on the lips. "Thank you, Avery," I murmur.

"For what?" she scrunches up her nose.

"For being here, for supporting me, for just being amazing." I hug her tightly and bury my face into her neck to breathe in her scent. Something about it seems to soothe me. I don't know if she wears a special lotion, perfume or soap, but I can't seem to get enough.

"Of course, 2, I wouldn't want to be anywhere else."

I smile and kiss her again in response. I have to admit, it feels fucking great to have someone in my corner.

Avery

"Shorty, let's make some sandwiches and hit the sack, okay?" he suggests and stands from the barstool.

"Yeah, that sounds good."

I follow slowly to the kitchen, my leg still healing and he prepares us each turkey and cheese sandwiches. He makes his with sloppy mayo and mine plain just as I like it. We eat standing in the middle of the kitchen like starving teenagers and he tugs me back to the bedroom.

Maybe it's time for round two.

I undress and climb into bed while he's brushing his teeth. I love when he walks around with his shirt off, doing regular tasks like brushing his teeth. He has no idea how sexy he is.

The toothpaste commercials have it all wrong. They should have a man like 2 Piece walk around shirtless, brushing his teeth and grumbling different things. They'd sell tons of toothbrushes and toothpaste. I'd definitely buy stock in that stuff.

He comes out yawning and the bed dips as he slides in next to me. His minds already going a million miles a minute, or else I'd be talking to him about everything prior to his sister's stuff happening. Strong arms wrap around me, pulling my body to his muscular chest.

We lie there silent and unmoving for what feels like an hour. He eventually falls asleep, never loosening his hold on me. It's the first time ever he's just held me and we've slept. I have to admit, I loved every second of it.

Sapphire Knight

I'm awoken by more pounding on the door. Is this going to be an everyday thing? Do people not sleep in around here? I mean it's a clubhouse; surely you'd think they'd all be hung over and sleeping.

"Yeah?" 2 croaks, and there's more pounding on the door.

I swear it better be a goddamn emergency at this rate. I get out of bed on automatic and run my hands down my body. *Yep, I have clothes on.*

2 Piece's sleeping on his stomach with half an ass cheek hanging out of the covers. I'm not too worried about it though, because it's covered with his tight, indigo-blue boxer briefs. Who'd have thought a badass biker would have colorful undies.

Opening the door about four inches, I peek through.

"What's up, Bean?" Niko grins happily, and I try to slam the door closed again but he stealthily slides his foot in before I can. "No-no, Bean. Time to wake and pack up," he grows serious, and the fog starts to clear out of my brain.

"Get the fuck out of here, Russian, she ain't going anywhere," 2 Piece mumbles grouchily.

Niko makes a face at me and I smirk. It's awesome for 2 to say I'm not leaving.

"What's going on, Niko?" I look him over; he's all freshened up and dressed.

He always smells like a million bucks with his delicious cologne. It wafts through the open doorway, and I inhale deeply. *Ah, so good.* I know, I'm a weirdo, but that's fine with me.

"Boss called. We're done, time to go home now. You go back to coffee and I go back to regular job with Boss."

He smiles widely and I lose my breath.

Go home now? But I'm not ready to go home yet.

"When exactly are you wanting to leave?" I reply, nearly in a whisper.

He stares, contemplating something silently for a moment. "We go when you pack."

Swallowing down my emotions, I hold my breath for a beat to get it together in my head. This is it. Time to pull my big girl panties on and leave the man I've grown to care so much for.

Who am I kidding; I freaking love him.

Turning around, I'm met with 2 Piece sitting up in bed, staring intently at me. I draw in a quick breath and utter the one thing I've been dreading since I've arrived. "It's time for me to go back home."

"Avery Marie," 2 grumbles, and I remain silent, still attempting to swallow my emotions away.

What's there to say at this point? I know he won't come to see me. He proved as much all the times before when I had to leave and wouldn't hear from him unless I came back to town. He's always let me know the score from the very beginning. I'm the one who's grown too attached and can't cope with the thoughts of not seeing him or touching him again for who knows how long.

I'm going to have to leave, to go home. I have to leave him not knowing if I'll ever see him again, and it's got me crumbling inside. Does he feel remotely close to what I do for him?

I get to go home, back to my boring life, to a job I hate. I'm going to go finish school, get my degree, eventually meet some mediocre man, settle down, and be unsatisfied for the rest of my life. That's if I even meet someone. I could end up a bitter old woman who sits home, lonely, emailing people their completed tax returns and looking forward to the latest *Price is Right* episode.

Niko clears his throat and we both glance to him. "He can bring you another time, if you wish? I do not like the sad Bean, chin up and cheer up."

He's brilliant. I wish 2 Piece would bring me later, but that's just not realistic. I mean, why would he waste time, energy, and gas just to drive me back after he gets sick of me? 2 already told me not to overanalyze stuff and to take it slow; while, in the meantime, I didn't get to analyze jack and discuss it with him.

"It's okay, Niko. I'll pack my stuff and not take too long, promise."

His face is painted with confusion, but nods anyway and I shut the door. I grab my bag and set it on the bed so I can get dressed and stuff my belongings in it.

I may as well just rip my heart out and leave it on the bed while I'm at it.

2 Piece

So, after everything we've gone through during her visit, she plans to just up and leave. I'm not finished with her ass yet, and she's fucking tripping if she thinks I won't fight for what I want. I said I wouldn't settle for just anyone coming around and I meant it. I'd damn sure take Avery, any day of the week.

Sitting up, I rub my hands over my scruffy face to wake up more. I need to shave; my beard's getting out of control. I normally keep it really short, but with all the shit going down, I've been preoccupied.

"Free bird, you aren't going anywhere."

"What do you mean?" Her gaze shoots up, hope dancing in her irises.

"I can't believe you'd just up and take off after you said you'd help me with shit. I told my sister you're my chick, and you are. I'm not ready for you to leave yet, I don't want you to go. Shit's been going real good with us. I'm not looking to cause problems by having you split town."

Reaching over, I grab her wrist and pull her towards me carefully. I don't want to hurt her leg. . She scoots over the bed until she's sitting next to me.

Lightly, I trail my finger over the side of her face and tuck her hair behind her ear. She nibbles on her fingernail, no doubt her head full of shit. I pull her hand away from her lips; I want to see every inch of her gorgeous face.

"What about you enjoying your freedom? I was trying to talk to you about this before and you told me to take it slow, not to analyze things. I haven't really been fretting over it, but now it's time for me to leave and I can do nothing but worry."

"Shh, Shorty, relax. You're my chick and that's all that matters, okay?"

She nods and blinks at me a few times. "Well, what happens when you get tired of me?"

"Avery, I'm not going anywhere and neither are you, damn it! You're so inquisitive, and I love that it makes you smart, but calm down, baby. If I get tired of you, then I'll leave you alone for twenty minutes until I miss you again. You're not about to go sixteen hours away, when I finally have you here and by my side, where you belong."

"You think I belong there, by your side, with you?" Her eyes become watery.

"Baby, you were made to be beside me and on the back of my bike." She gives me a brilliant smile and tackles me onto the bed. Tears trail down her cheeks and I wipe them gently with my fingers. "Good tears or bad?"

"No, they're totally good, happy tears. I was worried about being far away from you and not getting to see you. There's something I have to say first though."

"All right, shoot."

"Ugh, how do I say this? Geez." She takes a big breath and looks toward the ceiling.

I have to admit she has me a little worried, with all this baby talk that's been going on around the club. I damn sure am not ready to take that step. Well, maybe one day, but just not this soon. I mean, I would be happy if she were, but upset, too; it's just...well, I hope we get some more time together before we come to that bridge.

Eventually I wouldn't mind having one kid maybe, after we settle down some. Right now, I want to travel the country with her on my bike, make love to her wherever we see fit, and party our asses off if the mood strikes us. I'm a selfish bastard and want to hog her all to myself for a while.

She grasps my hand into her small, feminine one and stares me straight in the eyes. "Okay, so I'm kind of falling for you. I'm hooked and it's completely okay if you don't feel the same way; you should just know what's going on in my head. I want to be straight with you so we're on the same page." She keeps rambling on until I place my hand over her mouth. She tilts her head and scrunches up her forehead.

"Shush, woman. Of course, I feel the same way. I wouldn't be asking you to be by my side if I hadn't fallen for you."

"Fallen? As in, you already fell for me and you are currently in *fallen* with me?"

I start laughing loudly. She's nuts to doubt I wouldn't be absolutely crazy about her. "Yep, Shorty, I'm in *fallen* with you."

"So, you concede then?"

Damn rambling woman. "As in, have I given in to my feelings? When it comes to you, Avery, then the answer is yes. Is that good for you? Any other form of giving in is basically submission, and that's all on you, baby cakes."

"Oh, I'm down with that." She grins and I squeeze her to me.

"Good, then go tell ol' boy out there, that he's going home alone and you're staying with me. If you ever decide you want to go back there, and then I'll take you myself, okay?" I tip her chin up so she's looking in my eyes, while I let her know how serious this is.

"Okay, Silas." She smirks and I start tickling her on her ribs until she squeals.

"Oh, that's what that sigh was about yesterday, wasn't it?"

"Yes, I like your name; it's pretty sexy."

"Sexy, huh? Yeah well, just call me 2. I don't care if you call me Silas in here, but around everyone else, not so much."

I don't care for my name since it reminds me of my mother and living in California. I left that life behind long ago. I'm happy here and trying hard not to go backward.

"Okay, deal." She stands, wrapping her hands around my neck, lightly scratching it and giving me good chills.

"Hurry up and go tell him, so I can fuck that tight pussy." I smack her ass and she hightails it out of the bedroom with an exaggerated eye roll in my direction.

I'm glad we got that shit out of the way.

Avery

Leaving 2 for a few moments, I trek towards the bar to search Niko out. I can't believe 2 finally told me how he feels. I'm over the moon right now. I hope Niko understands. It's going to be so weird not seeing him several times a week like normal.

He's sitting on the stool, cheesing at me as I approach.

"Hey there, Russian beefcake." I greet and he chuckles.

"Spit it out, little coffee cake."

Taking a seat next to him, I smile. I love the names and expressions he's always coming up with, even if he does copy mine sometimes. I'm on cloud nine right now anyhow. He could call me a worm and I wouldn't care.

"Well, 2 Piece kind of made it clear he wants to keep me," I share excitably and take in his expression. He seems as if he was expecting this all along.

"Of course. He is dumb man, but not dumb enough to let you fly away."

I roll my eyes and scowl. "He isn't dumb."

"I believe so, but you — you love him, yes?"

I nod and stare at nothing in particular on the oak bar. It's true; I do love him. I never thought our relationship would grow into this. I never believed I'd need him to feel like I want to feel.

Running my nails in a few of the carved grooves, I can't help but think of what my mother would say if she saw me now and knew I feel like I *need* him. She'd lecture me on being realistic and growing up. I am grown, though. I know I don't really need him, but I don't want to think about not having him in my life either.

"Yes, I love him," I admit.

"I know this, man!" he cheers loudly, and I laugh at him again.

"Oh really, you know, huh?"

I rib him and he gets serious and says more intimately, "You look at him as if he is the only one able to cut your wings. That is good and sad." His eyes flash with something, and then meet mine again. "If he is no good, you call. I will be here in sixteen hours and I will fix him."

My eyes tear up and I groan. What is it with me crying so much here lately? I'm like an emotional goofball. I blink them back and lean in to hug him tightly.

"I love you, Nikoli," I whisper into his muscular shoulder. He always feels solid, so strong when I touch him.

He clasps me tightly, speaking close to my ear, "I love you, Bean. You will always be mine first. I just lend you to him."

The first tear runs across my nose and I try to suck it up. I have to be strong and show him I'm making the decision I want or he won't leave me.

"I know that, Niko, I envy the girl who'll capture your heart. I know you'll treat her like gold."

"Shit, gold? Nope, I will treat her as printyessa."

I know he's trying to lighten the mood for my benefit. It'll be so hard not having him close. Niko is fiercely loyal and caring. He's been a wonderful friend to me.

"Yeah, yeah, be safe and text me when you arrive." I shove myself off the stool and step a few paces away from him.

"I send picture of my bicep."

"Oh God, 2 Piece is going to love seeing your messages," I groan and shake my head.

"You know this!" He smirks as I backtrack to 2 Piece's room.

2 Piece

Three weeks later...

"I'm going with you guys, Silas," my sister argues stubbornly.

"The hell you are. You're seven months pregnant, and there's no way you can drive that entire way again by yourself. I told you we'd handle it."

"So, your girlfriend and Twist can ride with you, but I'm not even allowed to drive. Is that what you're saying?"

"Look, Sadie, just stay here. I don't know what kind of trouble we may run into, and I don't want you or the baby getting hurt."

"How can you possibly know that? You don't even know *who* you're looking for or what he even looks like!"

Twist approaches us as Sadie attempts the same argument she's been working on for the past few weeks. Twist and I talked it over with Prez. He had a good idea who this guy might be after hearing everything my sister said about him.

I already promised Avery a trip to Florida to meet her parents, so this has gradually turned into one big trip. First we'll go to Cali and then do some sight-seeing for Shorty. We'll end it in Florida, before coming back home.

When we get home; I think I'll officially ask her to be my ol' lady. She isn't too keen on the idea of labels, but, hopefully by then, she'll have changed her mind.

Twist wants to go badly. I've caught him and Sades hanging out a lot. I'm not real sure if I'm cool with that, but only time will tell. I can't imagine what he would want with my sister and her baby. I'm a little nervous with him being fucking warped on certain shit and chilling with my sister.

"Ready, brother?"

This is Avery's first long ride. I'm excited to have her with me.

Sadie steps in front of Twist, between us. "No, Silas, I'm going, damn it." Twist pulls her gently out of the way and attempts to calm her.

Climbing on my bike, Avery follows suit. I crank the engine as Twist climbs on his bike, still arguing with my sister. He shakes his head and tenderly places his hand on her cheek.

I'm not sticking around for that shit. I give my bike some gas, and we're off.

Avery

Two months later...

"Ohmygod London! You got a puppy, an adorable Doberman too."

Sitting in the middle of her living room floor, I let the little monster crawl and nibble all over me. I can't believe Cain got her and Jamison a puppy. I'm totally jealous; such a cute pup.

"Yes, he's a little asshole too. Not sweet like Muffin, must take after his momma."

"Wait, Muffin? What do you mean?"

"Well, I guess Tate and Cain had it all worked out as a surprise. Tate sent one of his goons up here after Muffin's baby momma had puppies."

I giggle at *baby momma*. Of course, she'd say that. Her and Cain are around each other way too much.

Ouch, little shit. I glance down and watch him climb all over my leg, trying to ferociously pull and bite at my jeans. "Jesus, how old is this little tiger?"

"He's twenty weeks old. Jamison thinks the puppy's the greatest thing in the world too. Cain calls him the *road dog* since he came all the way from Tennessee. His real name is Adonis. Thank Cain for that one too."

I burst out laughing and she follows suit. "That's hilarious. I can't believe you let Cain name him that."

"Chica, you know I don't let Cain do squat. That bullheaded man does what he wants!"

Speaking of, Cain and 2 Piece come walking into the living room with curious stares. He gives London a wet, chaste kiss then smiles mischievously. "What are y'all out here clucking about? All this damn giggling, we had to come check it out."

Laughing loudly thinking about the name again, I tease, "You named your dog Adonis? Vain much?"

2 Piece hears the name and chuckles, smirking at me.

"Ha trouble." Cain rolls his eyes. "Tell me, what'd you name your pup, if she were a girl?"

I smile wistfully and think about puppy names, while 2 Piece mean-mugs Cain.

"I think I'd call her Lily."

2 swaggers out of the room. I don't get it. It was just a name, not like we were talking about babies or anything.

London smirks at me knowingly, and I become even more confused. Cain snickers behind his hand and it starts to irritate me that I'm clearly out of the loop about something.

A moment later, 2 Piece comes back, carrying a sweet, sleeping puppy. She's black with tan markings and looks just like a baby, girly version of Tate and Emily's dog, Muffin. She's adorable.

He smiles softly and gently hands her over to me. "Meet Lily."

She yawns, opening big chocolate-brown eyes. I snuggle closer to her and she licks me on my nose. I'm assaulted with the wonderful smell of puppy breath and I'm hooked. I grin at 2 Piece gratefully.

"Well, Shorty, what do you think?"

"I think she's perfect. I've relinquished, not just for her, but for you. I love you 2."

Enjoy a sneak peek into Forsaken Control! XO, Sapphire

Ares...

I watch her laughing as he pushes her on the swing. She's always happy, smiling, and just beautiful. He's lucky he has her. Is it wrong that I watch him too? That I find him just as beautiful as I do her? He shouts something to her, and she giggles unabashedly; he smiles widely and it radiates happiness.

I want to feel like that. I want happiness too.

Her soft auburn waves blow in the breeze, giving me a full view of her sun-kissed skin. Whether I'm caressing it softly or grabbing it forcefully, I know it's soft. I've felt it glide through my fingers several times.

She was scared of me at first. I'm assuming because I'm not very friendly. How can I be friendly though? I'm the Enforcer. I'm meant to be mean, rough, and take care of things for the club. I love my job and my club; it's my perfect fit.

Now that we've spoken, she's not afraid of me anymore. She smiles and sometimes giggles when she passes by me. I love hearing her laugh; it brings me peace. I can't help but chuckle or grin each time.

He's been my friend for years and has never known that I'm attracted to him. I would do anything for him if he were to ask, but he never does. He thinks I like to watch a woman with him, when in reality, I only like watching him.

Now though...now he has her, and I want them both. I've never felt so torn before. I don't want them for just a fuck. I've had them for that. Not him completely, but we've been close. I dream of grasping his hair and thrusting into him roughly while I kiss her mouth. I doubt that fantasy will ever come true though.

She catches me watching them and flashes a bright smile, excitedly waving her hand at me. I grin and give her a slight wave back. He glances at me and smirks. He knows I like her, just not how much. He would probably kill me if he were to learn that they both own my heart. I wish I would have said something when they first started, then maybe I could at least have part of her too.

There's no telling what he or anyone in my club would say if they knew I find guys just as sexy as I do women. I don't generally give a fuck what anyone thinks, but I do value my brothers' opinions.

"You good, bro?" Cain comes to stand next to me, watching me as I gaze at them.

Blinking, I turn to him. "Yeah, I'm cool, man. Just enjoyin' this nice ass weather. You should bring your kid out." Cain is the one I'm closest to in the MC. He should be getting patched as an Enforcer soon also. It'll be nice sharing that title with him.

"Naw, London was talkin' bout givin' him a haircut and shit. She'll be here for the BBQ tomorrow though."

Nodding, I move my head to the side, popping the sore muscles in my neck. Fucking shitty sleep. "She's a fine ol' lady."

"Fuckin' right. Best bitch I ever met. What's up with them?" Cain nods toward the swings we had put in for the families. We say it's for them, but we all know the brothers really ordered the swings for Jamison, Cain's son. That kid is spoiled something fierce around here.

"Not a thing." Shrugging, I lift my chin toward them. "She wanted to swing, and he's wrapped around her finger."

"Yeah, that'll do it. I swear, London don't know some of the shit she could get me to do if she wanted." I nod, pretending to know what he means, when in reality no woman has ever had me like that. He claps me on the back. "It'll happen for you too, bro. Just give it time. It seems to be in the air lately."

No shit. Our crazy brother Twist, is busy following 2 Piece's sister, Sadie, around like a dog in heat. If she wasn't already knocked up, I'd swear she would be by him. There are more females around here than there ever has been before. I'm happy for everyone, honestly, but it would just be fuckin' nice if that shit happened to me too.

"I'm cool, man."

"Good. Well, Prez wants to talk to us 'bout some shit."

"He tell you what the fuck about?"

"Naw, man. You're the one he trusts over anybody else."

"Cain, your ass is gonna be an Enforcer before you know it." I smack his shoulder. "I'll enjoy sharin' the patch."

"I can't wait, bro."

"Let's see what the old man wants before he starts yellin' an' shit."

Cain grins and nods, following me into the clubhouse.

We stop outside of the office, and I peek my head in through the open doorway.

"Prez?" I call out and glance around the room, but it appears empty.

"Yep! Down here," he grumbles.

Entering the small room, I walk closer to his desk with Cain following suit. I peer over the desk because that's where his voice came from. He's lying on the ground, sprawled out with his long blond mop of hair in every direction as if he just woke up.

"Prez? What's goin' on?" I huff, shooting him a baffled look, instantly thinking he's hurt or something.

"I need y'all's help. Come over here." He gestures as Cain and I shuffle around his office chair, coming closer. I glance down at him puzzled. Has Prez lost his mind?

"Get down here, damn it!" He growls and we both bend down next to him. "There's a safe under here, but I can't get this fuckin' carpet to move an' I was tryin' not to cut it up," he says quietly, gesturing under his desk at the old, thin carpet. "I know everyone thinks the floors are all concrete an' shit, but I had a safe put in. That's what this ugly fuckin' rug's about."

Cain starts chuckling, and after a beat, I join in. He must feel as relieved as I do. "Prez, gotta admit, you had me wonderin' what the fuck you were up to for a sec," Cain chortles out, and I nod, agreeing with him.

"Me too," I reply gruffly, grinning.

"You guys both are gonna make me stroke the fuck out. Now give me a hand."

I stand back up and Cain mimics me; grasping one side of the desk, he follows suit. We move it across the room and Prez is able to finally get the carpet peeled back. He obviously wanted us for our muscle. I know he trusts me a lot to let me in on the secret safe, but he must be gaining confidence in Cain as well.

"Prez, maybe it's time for a different carpet. That shit's fuckin' rank," Cain mutters, scrunching his nose up in disgust.

"It's just crispy from all the bitches I've had bent over on it."

I shake my head and roll my eyes while Cain bursts out in a belly laugh. Prez never has any females in here. The man might as well be a saint in that department.

"More like you ate too many fuckin' nachos and that's leftover sour cream," I mumble and nod at the floor. Prez chuckles and shakes his head agreeing with me. "Is that all you needed us for, Prez?"

"Naw, both of you come back over here. I wanna show you where this shit is 'case sumthin' ever happens to me."

Cain and I shuffle closer. Prez is bent over a decent sized hole in the floor.

"What the fuck would be happenin' to you?" Cain voices the same thoughts coursing through *my* mind.

Prez is the closest thing I have to family besides my MC brothers. The bastard who raised me is no longer 'round, thank fuck. The no-good piece of shit who was supposed to be my mother got what was comin' to her too.

"Ares, you okay, man?" I blink a few times, clearing the unpleasant thoughts and glance to Prez. I don't know how long he was talking to me. If I think about those fucks, it's like it happened yesterday and sucks me back in.

"Yeah, Prez, I'm good. What's up?"

"I was tellin' y'all that ain't shit should be happening to me, but just in case. This is where the books and stuff is kept. All our dealin's—business-wise—and even the costs we spend on recreational shit. All that bull that went down with the Twisted Snakes not long ago got me thinkin' it would be easy for a big enough club to breach the compound. You two are the muscle of this club. I wanna rest easy knowin' you both know what needs protectin' if the five-oh or some rotten fucks show up. You feel me, son?"

"Gotcha. Ain't no worries, bro. You know we'll protect this club."

"I do know that. It's exactly why I wanted to include you both in this shit."

I look over at Cain, and he nods. I know he would die to protect his family, his club; so would I. Let's just hope it never comes to that.

We were dealing with some nasty shit when a club called the Twisted Snakes MC decided to start threatening the Prez's son, Brently. We eventually broke into their club, poisoned them all, and took them out to the pig farm not far from here. It got bloody, but the problem went away after that.

There's a knock on the office door, and we all pause, growing stiff because of the seriousness of the conversation. Cain and I step closer together to help hide the open floor behind us. No one should be around but club members, family, and the occasional club slut, but instinct has us doing our job of protecting.

I glance quickly at Prez and he nods, indicating for me to say something. Clearing my throat, I answer, "Yeah?"

She steps halfway into the doorway and glances at us, pausing briefly on me. Her lightly tanned skin calls to me, begging for me to caress it. She loves when I have my hands all over her...pulling, pinching, or spanking. I know she craves me just as much as I crave her.

"Umm, I was just checking to see if Prez had lunch or if he needs me to bring him something." Her voice causes my gut to tense. Her tone is silky smooth and feminine, the perfect combination to have any man hanging on to her every word.

Prez pops his head to the side of Cain's stocky legs so he can see her. "Thanks babe, but I'll be all right. I'll get something later."

"Are you sure? I can bring you something. I don't mind." She peers in at him innocently, and I swallow deeply as I take in her warm, honey colored eyes.

"Not now shug,' but I'll be out there later, I'm sure, wantin' some food."

She shoots him a friendly smile and nods. "Okay then." She briefly glances at us. "Boys," she acknowledges, nodding before she leaves the room. Releasing the breath I didn't realize I was holding, my stomach muscles finally relax.

"She's a sweet one, huh? Brother did good tyin' that one down." I nod at Prez but can't seem to make my mouth work. They all know I watch her. My brothers see how I look at her. Thank fuck no one talks about it, especially with the way these brothers around here like to gossip.

Cain reaches down and gives Prez his hand to help him up off the floor after he shuts the safe lid. "All right, I gotta head to the house to check on London and the kid. Little hellion almost caused her to shave off all of his hair the last time she cut it."

We all chuckle, remembering London's story of Jamison deciding to run after the dog right when she was trying to fade the sides of his hair. Then there's the time he thought the peanut butter was hair gel. He styled his little faux hawk with it, then smeared it over everything in the bathroom. That kid is something else; he's way too smart for his age.

Prez nods. "Give Momma some love, Cain. Take some of the stress off her, yeah?"

"Yeah, Prez, I got you."

He turns to me and fist bumps. "See ya, bro."

"Later."

"You want some grub, son?" Prez turns to me, blond eyebrow raised, after Cain is gone.

"No, thanks. I was gonna get a drink, unless you need me for sumthin'?"

"Nope. Shit's straight at the moment. You know I'll keep you informed."

"Yeah. How's Brently doing?"

He shrugs. "Just happy he's finally here, putting work in as a prospect. I'm happy to have my boy 'round the club where he belongs. Took him a long ass time to get here, but ain't gonna bitch now that he finally made it. How's he seem to you?"

"He doesn't talk much to me, that's why I was asking."

"Well, give it a little time, son. You're pretty cool with all the brothers. I'm sure he'll warm up. If not, he'll learn to, at least, respect ya'."

I grunt and follow Prez as we leave the office. He locks up, squeezing my shoulder as he pockets the key.

We head down the hall; he goes left toward the kitchen, and I veer toward the bar area over on the right. We're here at the clubhouse more than anyone else, so we're comfortable with each other. We're both the loners. We both fucked up our relationships with our old ladies.

I can't believe I even had an ol' lady in the first place with how fucked up I am inside. Poor bitch never had a damn chance with me in a relationship. Well, not past the fuckin'. She was young and dumb. I wasn't emotionally available to her, but I was always faithful. I knew I didn't love her, but I never let her feel unwanted. Then the cunt had to go whoring around to the MOBA, Mexican Outlaw Bikers Association, like those fucks even know what association means.

Walking behind the long bar, I snatch up a bottle of good whiskey and my usual tumbler. Lazy asses around here don't know how to wash shit, so I bought my own glass to use. I'm not going to drink after where some of their mouths have been.

I head to my usual booth. It's nice and worn. Pretty sure the cushion has my ass print permanently imbedded. It makes me look more normal size, like everyone else around here.

Placing the bottle and my tumbler on the table, I sit, slide to my spot, fill up my cup, and stretch my long legs out in front of me. I probably should have eaten with the Prez before I start drinking, but fuck it.

I take a few sips of the dark amber liquid, savoring the rich flavor as it goes down smoothly. It always makes the things I must do a little easier. I can beat someone to death if needed, then have some whiskey to dull my thoughts of it all.

The club door opens wide and sunlight pours in, briefly blinding me from the brightness, as Shay struts in. She's this hot little Italian piece I've had some fun with. Doesn't hurt that she's a stripper and can give me some good private shows. Seeing the woman I want but can't fully have running around here, it's good to have a piece strutting around that I can fuck with if I want to.

Shay scans the room until her gaze lands on me, trudging over. "Hi, Ares." She plops down in the booth right next to me.

I'm going to have to talk to Scratch about letting chicks through the gate before calling me or Cain. Brother hasn't a fuckin' clue about security precautions. A set of tits doesn't mean they aren't dangerous. Brother sees a rack and pretty much goes dumb.

I grunt in response, not really in the mood for her today. I just watched the woman I want to be with enjoying herself with another man. I'm not jealous of her being happy. I just wish I was a piece of it.

"Are you grouchy?" Shay wraps her fingers around the hard muscle of my bicep and peers up at me with a slightly wrinkled forehead, concern written on her features. It's about time I start pulling away from this bitch. She's getting way too comfortable, latching onto me and shit. Pussy is good to have around, but I'm not trying to get another chick like my fuckin' ex.

"Nope." I shrug, glance at her quickly, and turn away.

I'm met with laughter, and it sends a tingle down my spine. I know that laugh. *They* walk through the bar. *She* has her arm laced

270

through *his,* smiling happily. Of course, they're smiling. They're always fucking happy together.

"Brother!" he chortles, beaming a smile toward me, alongside hers.

"Yo."

"Goin' for a spin, you wanna come with?"

"No thanks, brother. Got some ass waiting," I grumble, and Shay giggles beside me, eating up the attention.

I shrug her off my arm, sit up, and take a long swallow of my whiskey. The gulp burns a little, but not much, being the seasoned drinker I am. I'm no alcoholic, but I've drunk my fair share.

"All right then, man. Have a good time."

I give him a two-finger salute, and he turns to leave. I briefly catch the glare *she* sends to Shay, her mouth stern and eyes shooting daggers, looking to kill.

I don't know why, but for some reason that little look makes me fucking stiff as a rod. My pants grow tight, and I shift my legs, thinking about taking her, about having them both right here in the bar, bending her over the bar top and eating her pussy while she sucks his cock.

They make their way outside, the club door slamming closed as they leave. A small hand caresses my leg, rubbing over my hard cock a few times and I growl, frustrated and fed up.

"You weren't kidding. You really are ready. You want it here or should we go to your room, daddy?" Shay questions excitedly.

"No, 'we' ain't headed nowhere, Shay. I wasn't talking about you and quit with the fuckin' daddy talk. I told you that shit ain't fuckin' cute."

"You're joking."

"Nope. Dead fuckin' serious."

She huffs. "Okay then, I guess this can happen another night."

Shay grabs her blue bag in a tiff, shouldering it and stands at the end of the table, hands on her hips, waiting. I glance up at her, eyebrow raised. "Well, should I come back in a few hours or make other plans?"

"Do what the fuck you want." I shrug, unconcerned.

"Fine, Ares. You have my number for when you're out of your bad mood." Shay spins, making her long dark brunette hair flail out in her wake.

Her gorgeous ass sways with her full hips as she heads back to the club door. She has a body made to taunt men, eliciting fantasies that will do nothing but get you in trouble. Too bad she doesn't fill my own fantasies. The door slams closed again as she stomps out. What is it with people always slammin' that fuckin' door?

I can't bring myself to care that she's upset. I know I should, but we first met by her dancing here. Shay was grinding all over my brothers and shit. I get it, that's her job and all, but any bitch I make mine won't be all up on every one of my brothers too. No one would have any respect for her after that shit.

Spin walks in from the back hall, heading straight for the bar. His ominous figure is decked out in jeans and a wife beater. He has his long black Mohawk in four big spikes up the center of his head, and his forehead is wrapped in a black bandanna. He has some sick ass tatts covering his arms.

He grabs a beer and swaggers toward me with a bored expression. Brother has some freaky ass eyes too. One of them is this weird violet-purple color and the other is grey. The guy has pussy swarming all over his tattoo shop wanting to be with him.

"You come in the back?" I question as he slides into the booth opposite me.

"Yep. Whatcha been up to?"

"Not a fucking thing. You?"

"Ain't shit. Shop was slow so I packed up early," he shrugs. "Wanna get inked?" He gestures with his chin to my knuckles. They always need touched up since I use them a lot. They're big and full of scars.

"Fuck yeah, let's do this."

"Bet."

"You know what? I feel like having a little party. You up for company?"

"Seriously, Ares? You know I'm down." He narrows his eyes at me. "I'm just surprised this is comin' from you." I nod and Spin pulls his phone out to start calling people up. I sit, nursing my whiskey, watching him send mass text messages to the brothers and God knows who else.

I get a good buzz going on and before I know it, people are piling through the club door. Marilyn Manson's "Tainted Love" gets turned up and there is laughter and booze everywhere. A blonde and redhead grind with each other in the middle of the bar's floor, rubbing their hands all over each other's bodies, leisurely pulling clothing items off. The brothers eat it up, sitting so we can easily watch them.

Spin has a scantily clad little Asian on his lap, kissing all over his neck. His mouth is parted slightly, and his crazy colored eyes are glazed over in pleasure as he harshly grips each of her thighs in his hands.

Twist, my blond MC brother who's covered in traditional tattoos, does a few lines off the table near him, trying to relax. I doubt it'll help, probably wind him up even more. That brother has demons worse than my own, I think. He'll most likely end up getting into it with someone tonight. That's how he usually works, and normally it'll be 2 Piece or a prospect. There for a bit I thought Twist and 2 Piece were going to end up killing each other. Twist saved 2 Piece's life a while back from a few members out of a different club, and since then, things between them have calmed down.

I take a long pull off the Budweiser Scratch brought me, damn near draining half of the bottle. When I set the bottle down, Shay is in front of me. She smirks mischievously, dressed in a short black skirt and grey sequin halter top.

London cuts in before Shay has a chance to open her mouth. "Go get my man a beer," she orders, then turns and sits on Cain's lap as he sits between Twist and me. London's all dolled up in her pinup girl attire—red lips, big hair, cat eyes, and fitted old-fashioned skirt, looking the perfect part next to Cain. I think they are the sexiest fuckin' couple I've ever seen. 2 Piece and Avery are hot, but London and Cain could be on a fuckin' Harley magazine cover.

Shay glares, obviously peeved, but does as she's told. As far as bitches go around here, you don't fuck with London. Every brother respects London and her devotion to the club.

"Cupcake," Twist chortles, leaning over as London gives him a small kiss on the cheek.

"Twizzler." London smiles at him and then turns to me. "Hey, big man."

"Yo." I chin lift and fist bump Cain at the same time. I don't touch London. None of us do besides Twist. He treats her like a little sister, and Cain would go fuckin' nuts if another male got that close her, good friend or not. He's fiercely devoted to London and his kid, Jamison. I respect the fuck outta him for it too.

"How's it, brother?"

"Good, man. I'm surprised so many people showed up." I throw my hand out, gesturing around the room.

"No shit, bro. No one ever hears 'Ares wants to party'. We all wanted to see what the fuck was goin' on." He chuckles and I grunt.

Shay hands London the beer for Cain and looks at me with her big puppy dog eyes. That shit doesn't work on me though. I ignore her as the club door opens, and I see 2 Piece and Avery walk in.

2 Piece scans the room, his eyes lighting up when they land on our little group. He tugs on Avery's hand, his weathered, tattooed skin clashing with her smooth and creamy complexion, leading her over to us. She looks happy to follow, her cheeks slightly flushed. She's wearing her signature daisy dukes with little lace shit around the bottom and a tank top. She has the best ass I've ever seen on a chick, both naked and with clothes on. Either she's warm from the Texas heat or he just got done fucking her, and I'm pretty goddamn jealous of that thought.

"Twist, Cain, Ares, 'sup?" 2 says as he pulls a seat up between me and Spin. Spin doesn't give a shit though; he's cool with 2 and fairly distracted by the Asian grinding on him.

I don't know if Avery really cares for Spin, though. Brother threatened to lock her ass in a closet when her Russian buddy Nikoli and 2 Piece were fighting over her awhile back. We all thought it was hilarious, but she was pretty fucking heated about it. Her man and her best friend going at each other's throats was enough for her to try to get people to jump in the middle. Spin schooled her really quick that around here we don't jump in on each other's shit unless it's absolutely necessary. The Oath Keepers MC is all about freedom and no judgment. If you can solve an issue with a few fists meeting flesh, then so fuckin' be it. Just one of the many things I love about the club.

Avery leans down, hugging London. They kiss each other on the lips, and I know the Brothers can't help but imagine what it would look like with the two of them together. Fuck! That shit would be off-the-chain hot.

Avery stands, then turns to me, her sweet scent hitting me full force with her movement. She grazes her soft petite palm on my cheek, rubbing my scruffy dark beard; I tilt my head and lean into it slightly.

She bends toward me, giving me a short, tender kiss on my lips. I swallow harshly when her lips meet mine, as feelings explode through my body, attempting to pull me under. My hands turn to fists as I clench my fingers tightly together to keep myself from pulling her to me.

After a bittersweet moment, she pulls back. Her lustful eyes are full of heat as she stares into mine, then she shifts her warm honey irises toward 2 Piece. Avery shoots me a small smile, resting her hands on my large shoulders as she leans back up. With one small squeeze to my shoulder, she releases me to sit on 2 Piece's lap.

I glance at him quickly to meet his gaze as he smirks knowingly. He knows exactly what she fucking does to men, and he loves it. His smirk makes me feel fucking stupid and I grit my teeth, trying to tamper down the beast inside, taunting me with memories.

My mother used to smirk at me a lot. Every time she would fuck someone in front of me, she'd have the same cocky little smirk painted on her worn face. A few specific memories stand out, always in the shadows, waiting to haunt me.

I remember her placed in the middle of the thin old blue rug. My mother's stringy black hair, frizzy and halfway torn out from her ponytail. Her black and blue knees on the floor spread apart, looking small and boney. The fat man who had just been fucking her earlier, holding his thick black leather belt wrapped tightly around her throat as he stood behind her, pulling it tighter and tighter through the bronze clasp.

He chuckled gleefully, his voice full of evil as she was unable to speak anymore, her face going from deep red to a bluish and then finally fading to an odd pale color. My mother's disgusting fake moans I was always forced to hear, finally cut off. I can still see her wide, empty brown eyes staring at me, almost pleading for me to do something. I sat in the corner, smirking, while I watched the life being drained from her.

I can't remember how old I was; life was very scary and confusing back then. I know she fucked a bunch of random men to make money, and she always ended up giving the money she received to my father. Not that my father was around much, and when he was, he was even harsher on me than she was. Fucking prick.

"You want another beer, Ares? Or how about I dance for you?" Shay pulls me from my last memory of my mother in the living room, by running her hand along my arm.

All these fucking couples around, and I sit here alone. Shay doesn't count. She'll jump all over someone else's dick in a heartbeat. It's probably for the best I'm alone, since I'm pretty fucked up. I wish I was a better man, but I enjoy being sinister a little too much. It helps me feed the demon lurking inside.

"Dance," I grunt as "Cowboy" by Kid Rock plays loudly and she smiles, seeming pleased I'm giving her my attention. Shay loves any attention she can get from men.

Her hips sway side to side with the beat, her skirt edging up slightly, just enough so that I can see the little crease at the bottom of her ass cheeks. My brothers and me all sit back and watch her. There's one thing Shay can do well and that's dance. Her sinful thighs part, giving sneak peeks of a purple scrap of material, barely covering her pussy.

She turns, facing me, rubbing her hands over her tits. Her bra straps fall off her shoulders and she sucks on her plump bottom lip.

I'm surprised when I feel a soft, petite hand in mine and fingers wind through my own. Clearing my throat, I glance over at Avery and she grins, her eyes alight with mischief. Reminds me of the very first time I met her. No one in the club really knew about her. 2 Piece had been sneaking her in his room so none of us had met her yet.

I was standing in the hallway next to the bar, chugging whiskey. There's a little closet, used to store kegs, with missing doors that I like to drink next to sometimes. I don't normally down liquor like that, but I was trying to chase away the fucking memories I battle with.

A door down the hall opens and "La Grange" by ZZ Top pours out of the room until the door shuts, silencing the hallway again. I turn away but I'm taken off guard when a hot little thing with Auburn hair and a nice thick, round booty walks past me.

My right arm darts out, snatching her before she gets too far away from me, and I slam her small body into the kegs as my large, rough hand rests around her throat.

"Who are you?" I growl so deeply you'd think I was fucking Batman or something.

"I'm Avery," she squeaks, the pulse in her throat fluttering like a scared butterfly under my fingers.

"Oh yeah? Is it my turn now, Avery?"

"I'm seeing 2 Piece."

"I get it. You a new club slut?" Relaxing my grip slightly so I don't crush the new toy, I lean in smelling her pretty brownish hair. It makes me think of fall with the red running through it. She's really well-manicured compared to the normal club whores around here.

I drop the whiskey bottle to the floor, running my now free hand over her right breast, across her ribs, and straight down into her tiny shorts.

I gaze at Avery sitting beside me now, as I remember staring into her wild eyes that night, how she looked as I thrusted my thick fingers into her hot, wet core.

They widen as I go in deep, my cock growing so fucking hard as she clamps down around my fingers, her body asking me to give it more.

I squeeze her dainty throat a little, loving the fact I can easily take her life; that I hold all of the power right in my hand. Her small fingers grasp onto my arm strongly, bright pink and purple nails digging deeply into my skin, as I pump in and out of her tightness a few times. The shit I could do to this bitch. She's so fucking responsive, I could make her melt in no time.

When she tries to speak I loosen my hand, her stuttering out, "No-no I'm not a whore, and I'm on-only seeing 2 Piece."

I drop my hand from her neck, pulling my fingers free as I back away from her. For fuck's sake, she *could* be my brother's girl, and I had no idea.

She stands still, her chest rising and falling rapidly as she huffs out a few breaths. I lightly flick over her erect nipple with the pad of my thumb, making her already rosy colored cheeks deepen further. I can't help it; she has on nothing but a goddamn plain white T-shirt and some small shorts with lace around the bottom. She might as well have stepped off the biker calendar hanging in the Prez's office.

"Sorry 'bout that, angel." Muttering, I gesture to the bar with my chin and she lets out a whoosh of air, turning to continue her trek to the bar on shaky legs. Guilt washes over me as I stare at her ass while she walks away.

Guilt, because even her being my brother's chick, I still want her something fierce. Even after finding *that* out, I *still* had to touch her nipple. I wanted to slip it in my mouth so fuckin' bad and bite it; I wanted to make her fucking scream for me.

Shaking my head, I walk to my own room, unsatisfied and angry, and slam the door. I can still remember that first taste I had of her on my tongue, when I had placed my fingers in my mouth. She was long gone when I had gotten to my room, but I savored her sweet flavor.

My lustful daze fades when Shay makes herself comfortable by plopping down on my lap, and Avery drops my hand like she was burned. No doubt Shay feels my erection; I'm hard from that memory of my run-in with Avery. Knowing Shay, she probably thinks it's from watching her dance, but that couldn't be further from the truth. Avery owns every hard inch of it.

Shay leans in and wraps her arms around my neck, pushing her breasts close to my face.

"The fuck, Shay?" I grumble, pulling my head back away from her cleavage.

"I feel it, baby...so glad you liked that dance." She wiggles, rotating her hips so her ass puts pressure on my dick.

"I told you nothing was happening tonight. I don't know how to be any clearer."

She glares and stands up angrily. "What the fuck are you going to do with your cock then? You already have a new bitch somewhere around here?" She looks around the room. "I don't see her right now." Shay's voice draws the attention of everyone and eyes shoot to us. I think the entire room hears me growl.

I stand swiftly, my metal chair flinging out behind me as I bellow, "Scratch! Come get this bitch now!" Her body slides off mine and she clutches my hand strongly in both of hers.

"No, baby. That's not necessary," Shay pleads. I step to the side, yanking my hand out of hers.

"You know the fucking rules, Shay." Pointing in her face, I drive my point in. "Go home."

"Ares, don't do this."

I gesture to Scratch and he comes scampering over quickly. "Get her the fuck out," I say. "No more bitches without approval."

"Okay, sorry about that, Ares."

Nodding, I turn, fixing my chair to sit back down.

"Fuck it. I'm out," I grumble loudly, to no one in general.

Instead of sitting, I head straight to my room. I don't have time to deal with any fuckin' drama. I'm too drunk at this point and I don't trust myself to not start up any shit with anyone. –Check out Forsaken Control for the rest!!!

Relinquish

STAY UP-TO-DATE WITH SAPPHIRE

www.facebook.com/AuthorSapphireKnight

Email

authorsapphireknight@yahoo.com

Website

www.authorsapphireknight.com

Facebook